"*I'd Like to See You Tonight.*"

Kitty was smiling.

Josh wished he knew what she was really thinking, wished he knew whether she would miss him as much as he knew he'd miss her. Although she was so difficult about this thing between them, he knew she cared. "You know, if we're not careful we could make a bad mistake."

"Such as?"

"Such as falling in love with each other."

Josh watched her closely for her reaction, but he was disappointed when he couldn't read her expression. Kitty's face gave away nothing as she replied with equal flippancy, "Surely we're too bright for that."

Dear Reader:

Nora Roberts, Tracy Sinclair, Jeanne Stephens, Carole Halston, Linda Howard. Are these authors familiar to you? We hope so, because they are just a few of our most popular authors who publish with Silhouette Special Edition each and every month. And the Special Edition list is changing to include new writers with fresh stories. It has been said that discovering a new author is like making a new friend. So during these next few months, be sure to look for books by Sandi Shane, Dorothy Glenn and other authors who have just written their first and second Special Editions, stories we hope you enjoy.

Choosing which Special Editions to publish each month is a pleasurable task, but not an easy one. We look for stories that are sophisticated, sensuous, touching, and great love stories, as well. These are the elements that make Silhouette Special Editions more romantic...and unique.

So we hope you'll find this Silhouette Special Edition just that—*Special*—and that the story finds a special place in your heart.

The Editors at Silhouette

SONDRA STANFORD
Cupid's Task

Silhouette Special Edition

Published by Silhouette Books New York

America's Publisher of Contemporary Romance

SILHOUETTE BOOKS
300 E. 42nd St., New York, N.Y. 10017

Copyright © 1985 by Sondra Stanford

Distributed by Pocket Books

ISBN: 0-373-09248-2

First Silhouette Books printing July 1985

10 9 8 7 6 5 4 3 2 1

America's Publisher of Contemporary Romance

Printed in the U.S.A.

SONDRA STANFORD
wrote advertising copy before trying her hand at romance fiction. Also an artist, she enjoys attending arts and crafts shows and browsing at flea markets. Many of her stories take place in Texas and Louisiana, where she has lived all her life, or in places she has visited. Sondra and her husband live happily with their two children in Corpus Christi, Texas.

Books by Sondra Stanford

Silhouette Romance

Golden Tide #6
Shadow of Love #25
Storm's End #35
No Trespassing #46
Long Winter's Night #58
And Then Came Dawn #88
Yesterday's Shadow #100
Whisper Wind #112
Tarnished Vows #131

Silhouette Special Edition

Silver Mist #7
Magnolia Moon #37
Sun Lover #55
Love's Gentle Chains #91
The Heart Knows Best #161
For All Time #187
A Corner of Heaven #210
Cupid's Task #248

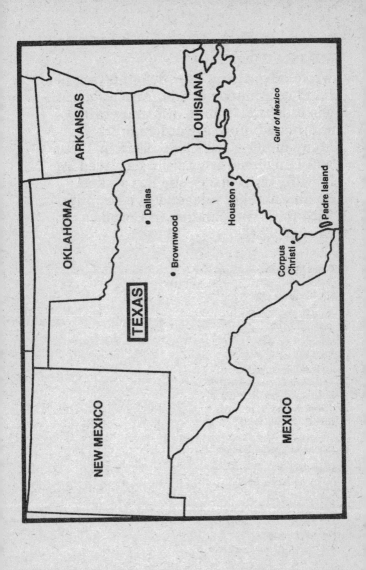

Chapter One

Joshua Steele crossed his arms and leaned against the doorframe, amused and appreciative of the scene before him. It was one to warm a man's heart on a frigid January night in Chicago at the end of a long, tedious journey.

"And three . . . and four . . . and . . . point those toes and straighten those knees and six and . . ." A woman's lilting voice chanted above the lively beat of a popular piece of music.

There were perhaps thirty people in the exercise class sprawled on the floor, waving arms and legs in the air. They varied from a terribly overweight teenager with pimples to a slender, attractive sixtyish woman with gray hair. They were all ages, sizes and shapes. They all wore leotards and they were all female.

Josh's grin widened as he watched their movements, some so awkward they were painful to observe, while others moved with the grace and ease of ballerinas.

In the latter category was the woman he'd come to see. Josh's gaze rested on her back as, oblivious to him, she led the class.

And what a back it was! Rich black hair was braided and pinned into a mound atop her head, revealing a delicate neck of milk white skin. She wore a cherry-colored leotard that hugged her body like a second skin, emphasizing the beauty of every inch it covered. Daintily curved shoulders and a narrow rib cage led down to the tiniest of waists before the body flared once more into exquisitely rounded hips. Her long shapely legs were sheathed in silky white tights. There was no conceivable way, Josh thought, that the front of her could measure up to the high standards of the back.

"Change positions and we'll do the other leg," she told her charges. With lithe elegance she smoothly swung her body around so that she could raise her left leg.

The shifting of the class members was less polished, and there was much shuffling and bumping. As they altered their positions, some of the women noticed Josh in the doorway.

"Okay, now, all together. One and . . . two and . . ."

There was a twitter of giggles. Josh was suddenly being looked over as thoroughly as he had been doing to the women a few moments ago. Because he had been equally guilty, he could scarcely get angry, but he did feel self-conscious over being scrutinized by thirty pairs of eyes.

The teacher, however, still had yet to see him. Though the class was now clearly distracted, she continued gamely. "And seven and eight and . . ."

By now the giggling had become open laughter.

Kitty Peterson gave up. She lowered her leg and shifted to a sitting position as she asked, "Mind letting me in on the joke?"

A stout woman in the first row grinned and pointed toward the door. Kitty twisted her head around, and for the first time she saw the man. Dressed in dark slacks and a tan coat lined with thick, fleecy sheepskin, he lounged against the doorframe as though he owned the place. His chestnut hair looked a bit unruly, and the grin that parted his lips was definitely unruly. It was openly mocking.

Kitty got quickly to her feet and strode toward him. "May I help you?" she asked in a frosty voice that was calculated to impress upon him the seriousness of his sin of trespassing. "We're trying to conduct a class here. A *private* class."

Unfortunately, he didn't seem the least bit conscious of his wrongdoing. He took his time uncrossing his arms and shifting his wide shoulder from the doorframe. He nodded lazily as though he had all evening to kill.

"A very interesting class, too," he said a little too heartily for Kitty's taste. His eyes, which now that she was near him Kitty could tell were a clear gray, focused on her. His gaze slowly traveled from her face right down to her toes and back up again, causing her face to burn as if with fever. "Down in Texas, I never had such a good-looking teacher when I was in school. If I had, I'm sure I'd have paid a lot more attention to my classwork."

In spite of her annoyance at his interruption, Kitty was no more immune to flattery than the next person. And besides, he was so darned good-looking! At five foot seven, she was no shorty, yet she felt small and ultrafeminine next to this man's towering height. His face was angular and long, with strong lines slashing on either side of his mouth and a forceful, squarish chin. A web of tiny, fine lines radiated outward from his eyes, evidence of a lot of squinting against the sun, and his skin color was a healthy golden brown.

A wicked, teasing grin played across his mouth, drawing her gaze. His lips were well defined and sensuously shaped, the sort of lips that probably excited a woman to passion by their kisses.

Horrified at the track her wayward thoughts had taken, Kitty caught herself. She fixed her own lips into a tight ball of sternness. What she had to do was be authoritative. "Can I do something for you?" she asked briskly.

"Now that," Josh said with a grin, "is a leading question. I can think of quite a number of things you could do for me, but you'd probably slap my face if I told you."

He couldn't seem to take his eyes off the vision

of loveliness that stood before him. He'd been so certain the front of her couldn't possibly equal the back, so he certainly hadn't expected it would far surpass it! The bone structure of her face, highlighted by the severity of her hairstyle, was delicately molded and refined; wide-spaced dark brown eyes surrounded by a forest of thick black eyelashes looked back at him with keen intelligence; her nose was small and straight, and her red lips were full and rounded and invitingly kissable—even while she puckered them in a ridiculous effort to appear firm and businesslike. Josh was having a devil of a time remembering he was here with a serious purpose.

Obviously the girl was not having the same problem. A frown lowered her dark eyebrows. "Look, I really am busy, so unless you have a legitimate reason for being here, I think you'd better leave."

She began to turn from him, but Josh lightly touched her arm. "Sorry." He was abruptly conscious again of the interested eyes of the entire class. "No more teasing," he promised. "I take it you're Katherine Peterson?"

Kitty nodded, tilting her head. "It seems you have the advantage."

"My name is Joshua Steele. May I speak to you in private?"

Kitty hesitated. "Is it important? My class is waiting for—"

"I know that, but yes, it is important."

Their gazes locked, his gray eyes with her

deep brown ones. The admiration Kitty had seen in his was still there, but it was overshadowed by something else, something serious. A twinge of anxiety shivered through her.

She wavered only a moment, then swung back to the class. "I have to step out for a few minutes. Eva, would you lead the exercises while I'm gone?"

The woman named Eva stepped forward as Kitty grabbed a towel and dabbed at the perspiration on her face. Then she draped it around her neck and followed Joshua Steele to the drafty entrance hall.

"All right," she said, turning toward the man. "I'm listening, but make it quick."

"I'm a neighbor as well as an employee of your father's," Josh explained. "I'm here to ask you to come to Texas and be a guest at his ranch for a few months. He would really like for the two of you to spend some time together."

Kitty stared at him, scarcely believing her ears. "You interrupted my class for that?" she demanded incredulously.

Joshua Steele's expression did not change; he reacted neither to the question nor to the blatant scorn in her voice.

His lack of response merely enhanced the anger that had wrapped swiftly around her like a cloak. Kitty no longer felt the cold air that pervaded the hallway. She burned with indignation. "Mark Winters must have more money to burn than I thought if he sent you all the way to Chicago just to issue an invitation I've already

refused! You wasted yourself a trip, Mr. Steele! I
have no intention of ever going to visit my
father." The emphasis on the last word was
unmistakably sarcastic.

"Why not?" The question was not an idle one.
Josh had wondered for years at the estrangement between Mark Winters and his only child.

Kitty's dark eyes glittered with fire. "The reasons are too numerous to mention. And besides,
I don't see that it's any of your business. Suffice
it to say I'm not going. I'm surprised he had the
nerve to think that by sending you here, he could
change my mind."

"What kind of daughter are you that you don't
want to see your own father?"

Kitty flinched beneath his harsh gaze, but
righteous anger reasserted itself quickly. No
matter what this man thought, she was not to
blame for the gulf between herself and her
father. Joshua Steele was crazy if he believed for
a minute that, just because he'd made a trip, she
was going to fall in meekly with Mark's wishes.
She wasn't in the least impressed by the fact
that, after all these years, Mark Winters had
suddenly remembered he happened to *have* a
daughter!

"I'm exactly the sort of daughter a man like
Mark Winters deserves," she answered frigidly.
"As far as I'm concerned, he doesn't even exist,
except on a movie screen! And now that we've
exhausted that subject, I have to get back to my
class. It's been nice meeting you, Mr. Steele."

"Not so fast," he grated. "And the name's

Josh." As she took a step past him, Josh's hand shot out and firmly clasped around her arm. They were now so close he could see Kitty's pupils dilate as she glared at him.

Anger and contempt burned their way through Josh. She was beautiful, all right, this daughter of Mark Winters; she was also cold and without a heart, exactly the sort of woman he'd learned through hard experience to avoid like the plague. Yet this one he couldn't ignore until his mission was accomplished.

"Let go of me . . . now," Kitty breathed ominously.

"Not until we've finished this discussion," Josh retorted.

"We have finished it!"

"You're a cold and unfeeling woman, and for the life of me, I can't figure why Mark wants to be reunited with an uncaring daughter like you. But he does, and I'm going to see that he gets his wish."

Kitty raised one black eyebrow. "Oh, really?" she asked sweetly. "Exactly how? Do you intend to kidnap me?"

Josh abruptly dropped her arm and, sighing raggedly, rubbed his neck. "I had hoped I could reason with you. The truth is, Mark is in serious condition in a Dallas hospital and he doesn't even know I'm here. If you care for him at all, I think you ought to go see him."

"What's the matter with him?" Kitty's anger, too, had abated somewhat, but the expression on her face was skeptical.

"His horse spooked and threw him off. Then

one of the horse's hooves came down on him. He has a broken leg and a punctured lung."

"Is this the truth?" Kitty asked warily.

Josh made an exasperated sound. "Why would I lie to you about something like that? Of course it's true. So . . . will you come?"

Kitty was silent for a moment. Josh could almost see the wheels turning inside her head. A strangely sad look·had come across her face, utterly at odds with the vehement anger she'd displayed a few minutes ago. He thought she was softening, so when she spoke again, he was stunned when she refused.

"There's no point in it," she said at last. "I'm sorry he's been injured, I really am, but it doesn't change anything. Except for the biological fact that links us together, Mark Winters is nothing to me nor I to him. I can't imagine that a visit from me would do either of us a bit of good."

"You can't be serious!" Josh exclaimed in angry amazement.

"I'm very serious," Kitty replied. Her calmness lent the words a quiet emphasis.

"Poor Mark," Josh murmured. "Poor, poor Mark. What a raw deal life handed him when it gave him you for a daughter."

Her dormant anger flared to life again. Kitty's eyes narrowed. "I'm the one who got the raw deal!" she declared. "Mark Winters doesn't know the meaning of the word *father*, so why should I pretend to be a loving daughter?"

Josh stared at her for another long moment. Kitty had the uncomfortable sensation that he felt he was looking at some strange species of life that was new to the world . . . new and distasteful.

Then he shrugged. "Suit yourself," he said indifferently. "Mark was disappointed when you turned down his invitation a few months ago, but at least he'll be spared a fresh disappointment since he doesn't know I'm here. Maybe he's luckier than he realizes."

With that cryptic comment, he nodded curtly and strode toward the door. When he pulled it open, frigid winter air swirled through the hallway, chilling Kitty to the bone. Or perhaps it was the man's harsh condemnation that chilled her.

Kitty slept badly that night. The next morning, picking her way past mounds of slushy, dirty snow, she still had Joshua Steele's disturbing visit—and her father—on her mind as she made her way toward the dress boutique where she worked. Her job at the exercise studio was only part time, two nights a week.

With the Christmas season over, the boutique was less than rushed. As she attached sale tags to merchandise the owner hoped to clear out, Kitty found still more time to think about her unexpected visitor the previous evening and the news that Mark was injured.

Joshua Steele obviously had a low opinion of her. He believed her to be a hard, brittle and unforgiving person, and strangely enough, that knowledge bothered her. When she analyzed herself, Kitty supposed that in a way he was right. But then, it was Mark himself who had made her the way she was.

All the same, there was the nagging thought that perhaps she was wrong to refuse to visit him. After another half-hour of wrestling with the dilemma and arriving at no firm conclusion, Kitty headed for the telephone in the stock room.

Fortunately, her mother was at home when she called and was free for lunch. Today Kitty felt a strong need to talk with her.

Jeanne Barnes was a handsome woman in her early fifties, and anyone noticing the two women together in the restaurant would have known at a glance that they were mother and daughter. Though Kitty's hair was long and Jeanne's short, Jeanne's hair was as dark as her daughter's. They also shared the same lively dark brown eyes and appealingly shaped lips. From Mark Winters, Kitty had inherited her height and rather stubborn chin, but the rest seemed pure Jeanne.

They enjoyed a close relationship, sincerely liking each other's company. The friendship between them had been strengthened by the fact that, during Kitty's growing-up years, there'd only been the two of them. And yet Kitty was sure it would have existed even if there had been an at-home father and other children, for they simply and genuinely took pleasure in each other's confidences and companionship.

No one could have been happier than Kitty when Jeanne Winters and Dr. David Barnes had married three years ago. After twenty-odd years of being a single parent, a working woman struggling to make ends meet while raising a child alone, her mother deserved to be rewarded with an adoring husband and a comfortable lifestyle. Kitty liked her stepfather and was grateful for the contentment he brought her mother.

Now, while waiting for their orders to be taken, they chatted casually about Kitty's job and David's suggestion that he and Jeanne take a February vacation to the Bahamas to get away from the cold.

After the waiter had gone, Jeanne said bluntly, "All right, darling, out with it. I could tell over the phone that this lunch wasn't just for fun."

That, to Kitty, was one of the bonuses of having a mother like Jeanne. You didn't have to tiptoe around or hem and haw about a subject. You could just dive into it. She leaned forward and dived.

"A man came to see me at the exercise studio last night. He said Mark was thrown by a horse and is in the hospital." It had been years since Kitty had referred to Mark as Daddy, even when speaking to her mother. Since the night she had graduated from high school, to be precise. "He wants me to go to Dallas to see him."

"Is he hurt badly?" Jeanne asked with genuine concern.

Kitty nodded. "He's in serious condition."

"Then you'd better go at once," Jeanne said decisively.

"Just like that?" Kitty's eyes widened. "Mom, that's ridiculous! I don't even know the man.

I'm not about to go rushing down to Texas to see a virtual stranger!"

"Listen to me, Katherine," Jeanne said in a stern voice of reprimand that Kitty hadn't heard her use since she was sixteen. "When all's said and done, Mark is still your father. He's your own flesh and blood, and you ought to have some sort of relationship with him." When Kitty would have protested, her mother held up a hand, silencing her. "I know it's his fault you haven't had that relationship before, but it's still not too late to remedy it. I honestly thought you were wrong a few months ago when you refused Mark's invitation to visit him, but I kept quiet because you are a grown woman, after all, with a right to make your own decisions. But this is different. He's seriously hurt, and if ever there was a time for you to reach out and bridge the gap between you, this is it. I want you to go."

Kitty's long hair swung in loose waves about her face and neck as she shook her head. "I can't believe this!" she said incredulously. "The man cheated on you, humiliated you, treated you like dirt, and yet you sound like a bleeding heart on his behalf. As a father he was a minus zero, too. After your divorce he never bothered to see me, he was never there for me, and here you are telling me *I'm* wrong for not wanting to see him now?"

Jeanne smiled sadly. "Yes, darling, I'm saying you're wrong. And too stubborn and inflexible. Much as I adore you, I am still your mother and I'm not blind to your faults. You take things too much to heart. You let the hard knocks prevent you from being open to the good things life can bring."

Kitty grimaced. "Are we talking about Mark or about Bob?"

"Both," her mother said promptly. "You had a rotten marriage, just as I did. But don't let that keep you from finding the right man and real love."

For some strange reason a picture of Josh Steele flashed into Kitty's mind, though why she would connect him with the mythical "right man" was beyond her comprehension. She'd found him physically attractive, sure, but what did that have to do with anything?

Frustrated at the intrusion, she picked up a teaspoon and began tapping it lightly against the white tablecloth. It was easy enough for her mother to talk from her current position. Jeanne was happy with her husband. The years had placed a blurring distance between her and her disastrous first marriage to the handsome film star who couldn't be faithful.

Jeanne had never told Kitty about Mark's cheating. Kitty had learned that all on her own when she was old enough to read movie magazines. In one article, which had chronicled the breakup of his second marriage due to his flagrant womanizing, there had also been a recap of the women he'd publicly dated while still in his first marriage, to Jeanne. Later on Kitty had read about the split with his third wife. That time the tables had been turned and Mark's wife had been the one to walk out on him.

Kitty's own husband hadn't bothered to be

faithful either. Only six months after the wedding, Bob Peterson had begun staying out nights, making lame excuses for his absences, and shortly thereafter the marriage was on the rocks.

That had been four years ago. Now, at twenty-six, Kitty was indeed a cynic. She had come to the conclusion that most men were born liars and cheats, and that only rarely was there one who could be trusted. She thought it highly unlikely that she would ever find a really good man like her mother's present husband. Men like David didn't grow on trees. The ones she'd met on the singles circuit were all wrapped up in themselves, their own desires, their own pleasures, the easy life without commitment. A woman would have to be crazy to get herself mixed up with a loser a second time.

Though Jeanne had tried, she still hadn't convinced Kitty to visit her father when, lunch over, she walked back to the boutique with her daughter.

When they reached the entrance, Kitty asked, "Want to come in and browse? We've got a lot of nice things on sale."

"I might as well while I'm here, though I don't suppose you've got any sundresses I could wear in Nassau, do you?"

Inside, a man stood at the counter talking with Kitty's employer, Angela. Kitty froze the instant she saw that tall figure, the broad shoulders in the heavy tan coat. It was Joshua Steele, a man she'd already thought about far more than she should have.

Angela spotted her and said, "Here's Kitty now."

Josh turned and their gazes collided in silent warfare. He walked slowly toward her and, without any pretense at polite preliminaries, said, "Mark developed severe breathing difficulties last night. His condition is worsening."

Jeanne gasped and Josh looked at her curiously.

Kitty said, "Mom, this is Joshua Steele, the man I told you about. Mr. Steele, my mother, Jeanne Barnes."

Josh inclined his head toward Jeanne. "The name's Josh. It's a pleasure, Mrs. Barnes, though I'm sorry it has to be under circumstances like this."

"Is he going to be all right?" Jeanne asked quickly.

Josh spread his hands and shrugged. "I wish I could be reassuring on that point, but the truth is, it doesn't sound very good." He reached inside his jacket, pulled out an airline folder and handed it to Kitty. "I took the liberty of buying you a plane ticket to Dallas. It leaves late this afternoon."

"You shouldn't have done that," Kitty objected, feeling pressured. "I can't just pick up and leave at a moment's notice! Besides, if Mark is as bad as you say, he's in no shape for visitors anyway."

To Kitty's faint surprise, this time Josh didn't attempt to argue with her. He just looked at her for a long time as though he were reading the record of her soul and found it black.

"It's immaterial to me whether you use that ticket or not," he said finally. "Frankly, I think Mark would be better off dying without seeing a daughter who's so eaten up with hate."

Abruptly, he gave a sharp nod in Jeanne's direction, then went out the door.

The silence was deafening, but at last Jeanne spoke. "Is he right, Kitty?" she asked gently. "Do you really hate your father?"

"I . . . I . . ." Confusion and shame swept over Kitty. Her throat was clogged with sudden tears, and she couldn't have spoken if her life had depended on it.

Jeanne tapped the airline ticket in Kitty's limp hand. "Use this," she urged. "If you don't go and Mark dies, you'll never forgive yourself."

Tears burned Kitty's eyes. She stared at a rack of dresses and all their colors ran together. But she wasn't sure whom the tears were for—the dangerously ill man who was struggling for his life, or the little girl who had once so desperately craved attention from her famous father.

Chapter Two

As always, the boarding process seemed chaotic and endless. Passengers straggled down the plane's aisles, searching for their seat numbers, juggling their carry-on luggage, some holding up everybody else's progress while they stashed coats or bags in overhead compartments.

Josh had been one of the first to board, having arrived early at the airport. He'd checked out of his hotel shortly after seeing Kitty Peterson, and there had been nowhere else he'd wished to go during the time remaining until his flight. Now he gazed beyond the empty window seat beside him—the seat he'd booked for Mark's daughter—at the depressing, gray winter afternoon. It would be dark soon.

He couldn't wait to get back to Texas. He always felt restless, hemmed in, whenever he

was in a large city. Of course, when he got back
to Dallas he'd be scarcely more comfortable
than here in Chicago, but at least it was more
familiar turf. There was no telling, though,
when he'd be able to get home to the ranch,
what with Mark in such serious condition.

His sense of failure was acute. His friendship
with Mark Winters ran deep, and Josh had been
determined to give the injured man the one
thing he desired most—a reunion with his
daughter. Now he couldn't deliver and he was
bitterly disappointed.

Josh had never known the Hollywood Mark
Winters and rarely even remembered that his
friend was, in fact, a celebrity. He'd been a boy
of seventeen when Mark had first entered his
life fourteen years ago. He'd bought Josh's father's ranch and, far from the glittering world of
moviemaking, Mark had shown himself to be a
no-nonsense, ordinary and responsible man who
wanted to succeed with the ranch and get along
with his neighbors. He'd had a direct and benefi-
cial influence on Josh's life ever since, and Josh
couldn't help but bristle whenever he thought of
Kitty's open disdain for a man he admired so
much.

He knew little of a movie star's opulent lifestyle, but he supposed that as a product of it,
Kitty was a typical spoiled brat who'd been
showered with all the good things it offered, only
to turn and bite the very hand that had fed her.

Josh got really steamed just thinking about
her. He was angry with her for coldheartedly
refusing to see her father, and even more furious

with himself because he'd found her so devastatingly attractive.

"Excuse me," said a breathless female voice, "but I believe that's my seat. Do you mind letting me in?"

Josh jerked his head around to stare unbelievingly at the woman who'd been dominating his thoughts. There stood Kitty Peterson in a heavy gray wool coat, a crimson wool scarf draped around her neck. Her long black hair fanned around her face, which was slightly flushed as though she'd been running. Josh's heart knocked against his rib cage.

He leaped to his feet. Eyes that a second ago had reflected the dismal gray afternoon suddenly glowed with warmth and a gladness he couldn't hide. "I'm happy you changed your mind," he said softly.

Kitty shrugged, and a teasing smile fascinated Josh as it danced across her lips. "I hated to waste the ticket."

Josh helped her out of her coat and stowed it in the overhead compartment while Kitty took her seat next to the window.

"We'll be taking off momentarily," a stewardess said over the loudspeaker. "Please take your seats and buckle your seat belts now."

Josh settled down beside Kitty. She was having difficulties with her seat belt, and after a moment's hesitation, he took over. Their hands touched fleetingly and a tiny electrical shock vibrated through Josh, amazing him. He bent his head lower, concentrating on the belt, and only when it was clasped at last did he look at her again. "I really am glad you've decided to see Mark," he said seriously.

Kitty's smile was nervous, as though the contact between them had disconcerted her, too. "I think I'm glad, too," she said, sounding unsure.

The plane was beginning to taxi.

"You almost didn't make it," Josh observed wryly.

"I know." Kitty sucked in a deep breath. "I was running through the airport like a sprinter in the Olympics."

Josh chuckled and the strain of tension between them eased.

The jet gathered momentum and, with engines screaming, lifted off the ground and into the bleak, somber sky.

When Josh glanced at Kitty once more, he noticed a white, strained look around her mouth. Her entire profile was rigid. Flying, especially takeoffs, affected some people that way. Josh supposed she was one of them. To take her mind off it, he asked the first question that popped into his head. "Have you ever been to Texas?"

Kitty shook her head. "I've done very little traveling at all. To tell the truth," she confided, "I've never been on a plane before today."

"No kidding!" Josh was genuinely astonished. The daughter of a rich man like Mark and she'd never even flown? It didn't jibe with his vision of the pampered only child of a star of Mark's stature. His curiosity spilled out. "I figured a movie star's daughter would have traveled all over the world."

Kitty's smile was wry. "Don't believe all the clichés about film stars' children. My life has been very un-Hollywood."

"Would you like something to drink, sir?"

They had been interrupted by the stewardess taking orders. Her smile for Josh was openly admiring. Kitty forgot her nervousness over being suspended in midair as she felt a twinge of dislike for the pretty blonde. Though in truth, she could scarcely blame the girl for flirting. Josh's rugged good looks were the sort that commanded any woman's attention. As he smiled back at the stewardess and spoke to her, Kitty couldn't help but think that such encounters were probably everyday affairs for him. Like other good-looking men, he could pick a new playmate any time he tired of the old one.

Of course, he could be married. She hadn't thought of that possibility until this very moment. Not that it mattered, she thought sourly. Any man as attractive as Joshua Steele would be bound to have his little outside flings, married or not. Just like Bob. Just like her father. Such men responded to the overtures of appealing and available women as naturally as a wild animal reacts during mating season—and trivial obstacles like marriage vows be damned.

Despite her brooding thoughts, she was somewhat gratified to notice that Josh did not follow up on the blatant invitation in the stewardess's eyes. He gave her a polite smile and responded to her questions, but otherwise he exhibited absolutely no interest in her. Maybe, just maybe, a tiny voice told Kitty, her unflattering opinion of him had been wrong.

They spoke little before their cocktails arrived. Josh seemed to have fallen into a reverie of his own, and Kitty was busy beating down her anxieties. She was far more alarmed about the news of Mark's worsening condition than she had let anyone observe—even her mother. Mark Winters might not qualify as her ideal candidate for a Father of the Year award, but Kitty didn't want him to die. By her own choice, she hadn't even spoken to him since she was seventeen; all the same, she couldn't imagine a world without him in it.

Her image of him had always been larger than life, no doubt a direct result of the many hours she'd spent viewing the strong and handsome actor on huge screens in darkened movie theaters. She'd seen him perform heroic deeds as the pilot of a fighter plane in World War II. He'd cleaned up graft and corruption in big-city streets in the States. His beautiful co-stars had always succumbed, falling in love with him on screen and often off. Whenever she'd watched one of his films, Kitty had always felt the same sensations—love, pride, adoration. Yet at the same time, a tight band of sadness and futile yearning would also squeeze around her chest. As far back as she could remember, she'd always been keenly aware that there was an emptiness in her life, a void that only Mark could fill.

Now a lump of something near panic rose in her throat at the thought of their imminent

meeting. What on earth could they possibly find
to say to each other? *How delightful to have this
opportunity to meet you at last*? Absurd! Their
relationship was too painfully close, yet also too
many light-years apart, for there to be anything
to discuss at all.

The drinks arrived, interrupting Kitty's unhappy musings. The stewardess did not linger
this time. There were too many other passengers
to serve.

Kitty sipped at her Bloody Mary, searching for
the courage to ask the question most on her
mind. Finally she turned to Josh and asked,
"What is Mark like?"

Josh looked at her over the rim of his glass of
scotch and soda. It was the oddest question he'd
ever been asked. "Don't you know?"

Kitty shook her head. "Please"—her voice was
husky—"tell me about him."

Josh saw that she was dead serious, and because of it, a dozen questions of his own leaped
to mind. But he didn't ask them. Instead, he
tried to reply honestly to hers. "Mark is probably
the finest man I've ever known." When frank
skepticism glowed from Kitty's eyes, Josh was
annoyed. "Look," he added gruffly. "You asked
me; I'm telling you."

Kitty lowered her gaze. "All right," she said in
a subdued voice. "Go on."

"I first met him right after I'd graduated from
high school. He bought my father's ranch. Dad
was happy enough to move away and be out
from under the burden of it, but I didn't want to
leave. I was born and raised there and ranching

was in my blood. Mark was still making movies and traveling a great deal then and had little time to spend on the ranch, so he hired me on as his foreman. That allowed me to continue living there while I attended classes at Howard Payne University in Brownwood. He even subsidized part of my college expenses." He didn't think it necessary to add that his alcoholic father hadn't given a damn about whether he got an education or not.

"How . . . how nice for you." Kitty almost choked over the words as unexpected and brutal pain splashed over her.

Josh looked at her sharply. He hadn't missed the bitter sound to her voice—as though she were actually *jealous* of him! He tried to assure himself he'd misread her feelings, but when he looked at her more closely and saw her rigid profile, the way she sat upright in a very tense position, he had to fight himself not to reach over and put his arms around her. He had an overwhelming desire to comfort her, though he had no idea why.

When he didn't immediately continue his story, Kitty said stiffly, "Go ahead. Do you still live on the ranch with him?"

Josh shook his head. "No. Now I have my own place a few miles away." He smiled deprecatingly. "It's not as large a spread as Mark's, but it's mine."

"Don't you resent it?" Kitty's dark eyes were wide with curiosity. "That Mark owns the land that should have been yours?"

"My father," Josh said slowly, "was going

through some tough times. The ranch was badly run down. If Mark hadn't come along and bought it when he did, the bank would have eventually foreclosed, so we still wouldn't have owned it anymore. As it was, Mark gave me the chance to stay there for a few more years, and when he decided to move in permanently, he lent me money to help purchase my own ranch."

"I see." Kitty was thoughtful. Josh was showing her a side of her father that she'd never dreamed existed. "And you're still his foreman?"

"No. When Mark moved to the ranch for good, he wanted to retire completely from all his other business ventures as well as from making films. I'm his business manager. I handle all his investment affairs. It means traveling fairly often, but whenever I do, Mark's ranch hands take care of things at my place, so the system works out well for everyone."

"Yes. It sounds like it."

"You asked what Mark is like," Josh went on huskily. "He's been like a father to me."

Kitty polished off the remainder of her Bloody Mary and suddenly wished she had a second one. "How nice for you." Bitterness crept into her voice again, making it sound hard as granite. "Maybe the reason Mark never cared about being *my* father was because I wasn't a son."

Josh could have bitten off his tongue. This girl really was sensitive about her relationship with Mark, more so than he'd first realized. Until now she'd hidden it beneath a cool layer of indifference and contempt.

"I'm sorry," he said. "I shouldn't have said that."

Kitty shrugged. "Don't worry about it. It's not your fault. My father's lack of interest in me dates back far before you came on the scene."

"How long has it been since you've seen Mark?" Josh asked curiously.

"Since his divorce from my mother. I was two years old at the time."

"You've never seen him in all these years?" Josh asked, stunned. "Why? Did your parents have one of those tug-of-war divorces, using you as a weapon?"

"Not at all." Kitty unflinchingly met his eyes and, in a voice devoid of any emotion, recited the facts. "Mark was simply too busy to spare any time for me. He was always too tied up with his next movie or the next woman in his life or his next overseas holiday. I was never on his list of priorities, you see."

"I had no idea," Josh said softly. "It's hard to believe, knowing Mark as I do."

"Well, it's true. A long time ago he killed any daughterly love I felt for him by starving it to death. That's why I can't pretend now that I care about him."

"But you're here. You're going to see him."

"Because I had a temporary mental aberration, obviously," Kitty retorted angrily. "When I get there I'll make my one obligatory visit to him and head back home as fast as I can. It's ridiculous and hypocritical for me to be wasting my time with a total stranger."

"Look, admittedly I don't know what went on

in the past or anything about your relationship with Mark, but don't you think you're being too hard on him? In the past few months he's mentioned to me several times how much he wants to see you and spend some time with you. I gathered there'd been some sort of estrangement, but maybe it's time for you to make a fresh start. Stick around awhile. Give the man a chance."

"A chance for what? To play the daddy role until the whim passes and he starts ignoring me again? No thanks!"

"Hard as nails, aren't you?" Josh observed, angry himself now. "Mark told me you'd been married once but that it had failed. I can sure see why. You don't even have a heart. I'm sure glad you're not *my* wife or daughter."

Hot blood surged to Kitty's cheeks. How dare this man presume to judge her! "You see precisely nothing," she said scathingly, "because you don't know what you're talking about! Let me tell you something. As critical and lacking in understanding as you are, I'm doubly delighted I'm not your wife! I pity the poor creature!" Kitty trembled with anger. Chewing on her lip to prevent further outbursts, she turned to stare out the window into the black depths of the night.

"Save your pity." Josh's voice was as sharp as a knife next to her ear. "There is no wife and there never will be. Most women don't have enough backbone and inner strength to be a rancher's wife. You," he added with contempt, "certainly could never make the grade."

Kitty looked at him with withering scorn, hot retorts burning her throat. But as a passenger walked past them, she bit back the words, remembering where they were. Surrounded by other people, they were compelled to remain sitting together in a tight space for the rest of the flight. Quarreling would only make it worse.

Josh's pickup truck was in the long-term parking lot at the Dallas–Fort Worth airport, so after they collected their luggage, they headed toward the hotel where Josh had called and made reservations.

They were both tired and sullenly silent as Josh took the freeway into the city. Kitty could tell little about what Dallas actually looked like —and, frankly, cared less—as the truck sped through the darkness. It had been a long and unsettling day and she longed for nothing so much as a hot bath and bed. The flight from Chicago, though smooth enough, had left her limp with exhaustion, physically and emotionally.

There was no question of visiting Mark tonight because it was so late. Josh had explained that a woman named Eleanor Robbins, a close friend and neighboring rancher, had been staying with him at the hospital night and day. But considering the strained relations between Kitty and Mark, a late-evening visit, even supposing Mark had rallied, would be unwise for his sake.

All the same, tired as she was, Kitty knew she wouldn't sleep without knowing his current condition. All through those hours in the air, she had been aware that there was a very real possibility that she could arrive too late, that Mark could die without ever knowing she had come. It was an unbearable thought.

She broke the heavy silence, betraying her concern with the unsteadiness in her voice. "Can we go to the hospital first, please? Not . . . not to see him or disturb him, but just to . . . to find out . . ." Her throat tightened and she found she couldn't go on.

She felt Josh's sharp gaze for a brief instant before he returned his attention to the freeway. Then, to her surprise, his hand found hers in the darkness and his voice was kinder than it had been since they'd first met. "I think we'd better check into our rooms first. As soon as we do, I'll call the hospital. If he's no better, I promise we'll go straight over."

Kitty nodded, having to be content with that, but she didn't speak. She couldn't. His sudden kindness was about to undo all her rigid control. She swallowed hard and stared unblinkingly at the neon lights that glowed against the night sky.

Forty minutes later they were in the hotel. Josh's room was two doors down from Kitty's. Neither of them bothered unpacking immediately. As soon as Josh had dropped off his luggage in his room, he returned to Kitty's.

While Josh put through the call to the hospital, Kitty sat on the bed beside him, tense and silent, her fingers laced together in her lap to keep them from trembling.

"Ellie?" Kitty almost jumped at the sound of

Josh's voice, even though it was low. "Josh here. How is he?" Kitty stared at Josh's profile, trying to read the news from his expression, but his face gave away nothing and neither did his words. "Yes. Um-hum, I see. Yes, she's here. What? No, I'll leave that up to you. Right. Okay. Call me if there's a change."

Kitty was almost beside herself by the time Josh cradled the phone and turned to her. "Mark's much better," he said, grinning. "The doctors think the worst has passed."

Without any idea that she was about to do it, Kitty burst into sobs. "I'm so . . . I'm so . . . happy."

"Hey, hey," Josh murmured softly. "It's all right now." Instinctively he did the only thing he knew to do. He wrapped his arms around her and held her close. Kitty's head bent to his shoulder and her entire body trembled as he stroked her hair. "There's no need for tears now. He's going to be fine."

Kitty sniffed and her voice was muffled against his shoulder. "I'm sorry. I didn't mean to . . ." She tried to pull back, but Josh wouldn't let her. Instead, his arms tightened about her, his body infusing warmth into hers. His cheek was pressed against her head and she could feel his fingers weaving through her hair.

"Shhhhh," Josh whispered. "Just relax. Everything's going to be all right."

Somehow, she believed him. She felt so safe, so secure. His broad chest was warm and strong, as though it were built just for this, just for her solace. She couldn't remember ever being consoled by any man before, not even by her husband, Bob, and she was loath to leave the sanctuary offered by this man's embrace. Weakly, Kitty surrendered to the soothing comfort of his words and the infinitely sweet sensation of his sheltering arms.

Josh could not recall ever having more tender feelings toward any woman than he did at this moment for the slender woman he held. The scent of her was enticing, like a faint drift of roses, and her body, snuggled so close to his, was soft and alluring. Her hair was silky under his touch, and as he pressed his face against it, he felt unexpected hot desire leap into his veins.

At last Kitty pulled back and Josh handed her his handkerchief. She mopped at her moist eyes and gently blew her nose. "I don't know what came over me," she apologized, not daring to meet Josh's gaze. "I seldom cry. Why I should have treated you to such an emotional breakdown, I can't imagine. Please, forgive me."

"Don't be silly." Because she wouldn't look at him, Josh put a finger beneath her chin and lifted her face. His smile was gentle. "It just proves you're human like everyone else, even though you didn't want me to see that. It just goes to show that you do care about Mark after all. Why," he asked, a teasing light in his eyes, "did you try to pretend otherwise?"

Kitty couldn't answer. It wasn't expected anyway. As their eyes met, something inexplicable had happened. Some force, strong and inexorable, had overshadowed everything else. She was mesmerized by the soft glow in his eyes, by the nearness of him, by those firm yet tender lips.

Josh's gaze drank in the details of her face. Her beautiful chocolate-colored eyes, still damp from her tears, were wide and luminous; her hair, slightly mussed from his hand's gentle comforting, shone like midnight; her skin was fine and smooth, an open invitation to a man's hand to stroke it. But it was her lips that fascinated him most. They were soft and full and slightly parted, as though by surprise. And perhaps that was so, for he was surprised himself at how very much he wished to kiss her. Forgotten now was his initial resistance to her attraction; forgotten, too, was his anger. Nothing seemed to matter anymore except that she was here, still lightly held in his arms, and that he was a man and she was a woman.

Slowly he drew her closer, and she did not resist. Josh looked deeply into her eyes for one brief instant before he gave in to temptation. With deliberation, he bent his head and touched her lips with his.

Kitty did not have time to analyze why she wanted Josh to kiss her. Her mind wasn't working properly in any case. She was all feeling, all sensation, and just now she knew only that she wanted his kiss more than anything in the world.

All the same, she was unprepared for the powerful devastation it wrought. A sudden conflagration spread through her, wild and untamed, as his mouth parted her lips and his

tongue sought to know her. Josh crushed her to
him fiercely and their hearts thundered in
rhythm. A hungering passion utterly consumed
her, matching an urgency she could sense in
him.

Josh lost himself in the sweet pleasure of her.
Her lips were warm and yielding; her body soft
and pliable. His hands stroked her head, her
hair, the curve of her back and down to her hips,
and still he pressed her closer. Kitty's hands,
hesitant at first, had crept up his arms, clung to
his shoulders and finally curved around his
neck. Her breathing was as erratic as his own,
and her response intensified the white-hot fire of
his own desire.

Without even being conscious of it, he drew
her down until she lay across the bed. He bent
over her, raining kisses upon her face while his
hands followed the exciting contours of her
body.

Kitty began to ache with a need she had long
suppressed beneath layers of ice-hard restraint.
Her fingers began to explore Josh's strong back,
learning the corded muscles, his broad shoulders, the radiant warmth of his neck and face.
Her pulses clamored as his kisses searched out
her eyelids, her brows, her cheekbones, her chin
and, once again, her lips.

Exquisite sensations streaked through her
when Josh's hand found and caressed her
breast. The ache inside her built, more powerful, more painful with each passing second. A
deliciously numbing languor stole over her as

she gave herself up totally to the dizzying spirals of ecstasy he brought to her.

Yet it wasn't enough for either of them. Their appetites had merely been whetted—no banquet had yet satisfied their hunger; no wine had quenched their thirst.

Josh became impatient first. He withdrew slightly so that his hands could move between them to the center of her blouse. He opened one button, paused to kiss her throat, and was about to open the next when Kitty's hand stopped him.

"No," she rasped.

Josh's fingers stilled. He lifted his gaze to her face. His eyes were dark and slumberous, glazed with unmistakable desire. His full, sensual lips pressed together as he looked at her mutely.

"This . . . this is crazy, don't you see?" Kitty pleaded.

"Is it?"

There was no anger in his voice. *That* she could have handled easier; rather, there was profound disappointment, as though she had hurt him somehow, right down to his soul.

"Yes, of course it is," she insisted, though even to her own ears she didn't sound too confident. She pushed his hands away and struggled to wriggle out from beneath his massive chest. Her breathing was heavy; she was close to tears again—she, who rarely cried! "We . . . we're strangers. We can't possibly be d-doing this!"

There was the smallest of silences, yet Kitty could feel the tension in Josh. "You're right," he said then, swinging to his feet. "It is crazy.

We've both been rocked off-balance today, that's all. Forget it ever happened. I already have."

In two strides he was at the door.

Kitty stared at the floor until she heard the soft click of the closing door. Only then did she lift her head and stare at it through a rainbow of tears.

Damn tears! She turned back to the bed and savagely pounded the pillow.

Chapter Three

For the second night in a row, Kitty slept badly. She was up at dawn, but even a leisurely shower did not perform its usual miracle of giving her a sense of well-being. She stood before the large bathroom mirror applying her makeup and came to the unhappy conclusion that she'd never looked worse in her life.

"Fine day for meeting your father," she said snippishly to her scowling reflection. "One look at this ugly mug and it'll be another twenty-four years before he'll ever want to see it again."

She dreaded facing Josh Steele this morning as much as confronting Mark. After the mistake of last night, she didn't know how she would be able to meet his eyes. The feelings she'd had when he'd held her and kissed her! Hot shame washed over her at the memory.

In an effort to run away from her grim thoughts and fears, Kitty dressed hastily in a dark blue wool skirt and a pale blue sweater and, as soon as she was ready, went downstairs to find the coffee shop. It was still far too early to visit the hospital, and Josh probably wasn't even awake yet. She doubted that *he* had lain awake half the night regretting what had happened between them!

In the lobby she bought a newspaper before entering the almost deserted coffee shop. She settled at a small table near the door, ordered coffee and scanned the headlines, but after about ten minutes she realized she hadn't absorbed a single word. She was too anxious about the day that lay ahead.

She didn't notice Josh until he was actually standing beside the table. "Mind if I join you?" he asked.

Kitty looked up in surprise. He appeared fresh and well rested and was neatly dressed in dark slacks and a beige sweater-knit shirt that hugged his shoulders and chest. His potent sexuality seemed to scream out at her, once more disturbing her senses. Quickly, she shifted her gaze from him back to her newspaper and swallowed hard. "Of course not," she said in a hollow voice. As he took the seat across from her, she added in a more normal tone, "I didn't expect you'd be awake yet."

"I'm a country boy," he reminded her. "I'm used to getting up early. Somehow I didn't think a city girl would be such an early riser, though."

Kitty caught the sharp edge of his voice. She

lifted her head and glowered at him. "I never heard of a law giving country people a monopoly on mornings," she snapped.

Josh laughed, inordinately pleased that he'd annoyed her. Last night she'd played hell with his emotions and he wouldn't easily forgive that. He had no intention of getting mixed up with Mark Winter's daughter. So far, he didn't think she was much of a bargain as a daughter, and she sure wasn't what he needed in the romance department. So much the better if he made her dislike him. That would be a lot easier to handle than having her go soft and sweet and melt in his arms.

All the same, his eyes were busy absorbing the pleasing picture she made this morning. The sky blue color of her sweater was most becoming to her milk white complexion and jet black hair, and the soft clinging wool curved delightfully over her full breasts. Lord, he thought in despair as he forced himself to drag his gaze away, why did she have to be so beautiful?

Choosing to ignore her barbed comment, he said, "Ellie called from the hospital a few minutes ago."

"And?" He saw Kitty's jaw tense.

"Mark had a very restful night and seems much stronger this morning." He didn't miss seeing the tension ooze from her, subtle as the change was. "Of course, it's too early yet for the doctor to make his rounds, but Ellie feels so confident that the worst is over, she's decided to go home this morning, now that we're here."

Kitty's throat suddenly felt dry. "Does my

father know that I . . . that we're here? I can't just walk in and surprise him. The shock . . ."

"He knows," Josh reassured her. "Ellie told him, so he's expecting you."

There seemed little to say after that. Kitty fell silent and so did Josh. He seemed as wary of her this morning as she was of him. It was awkward, this pretense that nothing had happened between them last night, and yet it was the only possible way to go forward. Kitty was relieved when the waitress brought the breakfast menus.

Throughout the meal, and afterward on the drive to the hospital, the strain between them remained. They talked, but only in careful, polite monosyllables. There was no real conversation. The more they tried to behave normally, the more awkward the situation seemed.

Kitty's nerves were almost shattered by the time they reached the hospital. Her legs felt wooden as she walked beside Josh through the maze of polished corridors. The antiseptic scent was numbing, and her steps grew slower.

When Josh realized she hadn't kept up with him, he paused. "It's just a couple of doors down and . . ." Seeing the strange expression on her face, he asked sharply, "What's wrong?"

Kitty struggled to find her voice. "I . . . can't," she said weakly. "I can't go through with this."

Josh's face darkened with instant fury. "You came all this way and now you're going to back out?" He shook his head. "I won't let you!" He grabbed her arm roughly and propelled her forward until they reached a closed door. "This," he added gruffly, pointing at it, "is his room, and he's waiting to see you. Now get in there!"

Kitty's eyes blurred as she gazed at the door. The man on the other side of it was her father, yet he was also a virtual stranger. For her, Mark Winters was a face on a movie screen, a typewritten letter done by a secretary with only his signature hastily scrawled across the bottom. He was an occasional voice on the telephone, and even *that* she hadn't heard in years. How could she possibly go in there and pretend anything existed between them? Nothing bound them except biology.

"I can't pretend," she said shakily, "to be his loving, long-lost daughter. It would be a lie and the worst form of hypocrisy. I should never have come." She turned and took a step away.

Josh's fingers dug into her shoulder as he swung her around. His eyes were expressive with anger and accusation. "The truth is," he said harshly, "you're selfish and a coward!"

"That isn't so!" Kitty jerked away from him. "You have no right to judge me."

Relentlessly, he went on. "You're selfish because you'd rather dwell on past grievances than bury the hatchet, even now! You're a coward because you haven't got what it takes to get beyond all that and make a new beginning."

Kitty was speechless with fury. She hated Josh for his cruel words, for his lack of compassion toward her side of things. All her life she'd been denied a real father because the man on the other side of that door had been supremely indif-

ferent toward her, yet Joshua Steele had the gall
to call *her* selfish and a coward.

She went hot, then cold with rage, but finally
the anger suffusing her was so strong that it
overcame her reluctance. Without stopping to
consider that this was precisely what Josh had
had in mind, she pushed open the door and
stepped inside the room.

There was little about the face before her that
resembled the handsome, famous face that for
years had smiled at Kitty from movie and TV
screens or magazine pages. This was but a
pitiful shell of that once magnificent, virile hero
who had thrilled the hearts of millions.

Mark Winters's eyes were closed, and his head
rested wearily against the pillows. For a suspended moment, Kitty's heart was in her throat
as she absorbed the sight of this person who
happened to be her father. His thick dark hair
was thinning now and almost completely silver;
the ruggedly etched plains of his face had become sharp and gaunt. Age lines creased his
forehead and webbed his cheeks, and the for-
merly healthy complexion was sallow. Judging
by his shoulders, arms and hands, visible above
the bedcovers, he weighed much less than the
man she'd seen on film.

His right leg was elevated and in a cast; gray
oxygen tubes were inserted into his nostrils, and
an I.V. was connected to a vein in his left arm.

Kitty was deeply shocked at how still he was
and how very ill he looked. Josh had told her so,
and she'd thought she was mentally prepared for
it, but the reality of seeing him this way was

terrifying. Fear sped through her, and she wondered if she had, after all, been too late. She turned jerkily toward Josh, who had followed her into the room, her eyes speaking the dreaded question. But her attention was drawn back to the bed by that familiar, distinctive voice.

"So you did come. I didn't really believe you would."

Kitty turned back and her gaze boldly met her father's. Only his incredibly beautiful lake blue eyes had not changed with the years. They were still as keen and penetrating as they'd ever been in Technicolor. Just now they were somber and assessing.

She stepped forward and nodded. "Hello, Mark. I almost *didn't* come," she said bluntly.

Mark Winters managed a wan smile. "At least you're honest."

Kitty tilted her head. "Would you rather I lied to you?" she challenged.

Mark made a negative motion with his head, but his gaze never once left hers. "No," he said softly. "You've come and that's enough. I don't want there to be pretense between us."

Kitty nodded. Her voice was devoid of any emotion. "That's what I thought, too."

"I think I'll go downstairs and grab a cup of coffee," Josh said.

Neither of them noticed as he slipped quietly out of the room and closed the door behind him. They were too intent on each other. For a long time father and daughter were silent, each frankly assessing and studying the face of a familiar stranger. There was no softening in either of them, no attempt to display false affection or sentimentality. There were only questions in their eyes and a wariness on both sides.

At last Kitty broke the lengthening silence. "They tell me you've had a very rough time of it," she said quietly. "How are you feeling?"

"Compared to the past couple of days, I feel terrific this morning," Mark replied. He waved vaguely toward a chair and said, "Sit down."

Kitty pulled a chair near the bed. When she was seated and looked toward Mark again, she saw that a faint ghost of a smile played across his dry lips. "You've grown into a very beautiful woman, Kitten," he said, using the nickname he'd always called her.

Kitty felt a lump swell in her throat. No one else had ever called her that. When she was young, it had seemed to her a very special name, an endearment that bonded her close to Mark through his letters and phone calls and helped her in her illusion that her father did love her, that soon he would visit her. But it had never happened, and in time she had learned to hate the name. Now, surprisingly, hearing him say it melted something inside of her.

"Thanks," she said brusquely, trying to hide the emotion that had so unexpectedly come over her. "People tell me I take after Mother, which to me is a high compliment."

Mark's head made a small movement that simulated a nod. "You do look like her." There was a little pause, and then he asked, "How is Jeanne?"

"Fine. She stays very active in volunteer organizations and she's very happy in her marriage."

If there was a certain accusation in her last statement, Mark ignored it. Mildly, he said, "I'm glad for her. Very glad. She's a wonderful woman."

Kitty nodded. "Yes," she agreed. "She's the best. You know, if it hadn't been for her, I wouldn't be sitting here right now. She convinced me to come see you."

Mark's eyebrows rose. She had managed to genuinely surprise him. "No kidding? I figured Josh must've sweet-talked you into it."

Kitty pressed her lips tightly together, her annoyance obvious. "Joshua Steele and I don't get along," she stated flatly. But because she didn't want to go further into that subject, she went on hastily, "By the way, Mom sends her best wishes for your recovery."

An odd light flickered in Mark's eyes. He turned his head and looked away from Kitty, and for a long time he was silent. At last he looked at her again and said softly, "Well, that's more than I deserve from Jeanne. What about you? Do I have your best wishes too?"

Kitty shrugged. "I'm here, aren't I?"

"Begrudgingly, I think," Mark retorted. "But I guess in a way you have a lot more to forgive than your mother does, don't you?"

Kitty shrugged again. "I'd say it was a toss-up." She saw Mark wince at that and was at once ashamed of herself. It wasn't like her to be quite so outspoken with anyone, but the old resentments ran deep. They had been bottled up inside, building layer upon layer through the years, and they weren't easy to conceal now that she was finally face-to-face with her father. Yet he was a very sick man and this was definitely not the time to air her animosities. "I'm sorry," she said contritely. "I shouldn't have said that."

"It's okay," Mark told her. "I had it coming. That and a whole lot more." He shifted his position just a fraction and grimaced. "Damn it, they've got me so hog-tied in this bed I can hardly move an inch. Don't ever let a horse fall on you, Kitten. It's the pits."

In spite of herself, Kitty grinned in sympathy. "I don't suppose I'm in much danger of that in Chicago. Being run down by traffic is a distinct possibility, but I'm not too worried about horses."

"You're going to spend some time at my ranch, aren't you?" Mark asked. There was a fire of eagerness in his blue gaze. "You don't have to go horseback riding, of course, but you could if you want. What happened to me was just a freak accident. I don't want to scare you off."

"I'm not scared," she assured him. "But I don't imagine there'll be time to see your ranch, much less ride horses. I can only be away from my job a week or two at the most, and I intend to stay right here in Dallas so I can visit you." The forlorn expression that came to Mark's face made Kitty wish a different answer had been possible.

"I was hoping you'd stay a few months like I asked you to before, so we could really have time to get acquainted," he said slowly. "After all these years, a week or two isn't much. And that's assuming," he added glumly, "I fool the doctors and ever get out of this place alive and go home myself."

"I won't listen to talk like that," Kitty said sharply. "Of course you'll be going home. You're going to be fine. It just may take a little while, that's all."

Mark went very still, and the blue eyes darkened as he stared at her intensely. "You *do* care, after all," he said shakily.

Kitty bristled and sat up straighter. "Well, of course I do!" she exclaimed. "In exactly the same way I'd be concerned for an injured stray dog."

Mark broke the heaviness of the moment by laughing abruptly. They both knew better, both knew the truth, but the underlying sentiments were best left unspoken.

Suddenly he coughed, his expression turning to pain, and Kitty was instantly alarmed. She jumped to her feet and stepped to the bed to bend over him. "Are you all right, Mark?" she asked anxiously. "Should I call a nurse?"

Mark shook his head. "No," he said weakly. "I'll be all right. I just shouldn't have laughed."

Kitty was not at all reassured and was silently debating whether to ring for a nurse over his objections when the door opened behind her. She swung around eagerly, hoping it was a nurse, but instead it was Josh.

"The nurses told me we need to leave now," he said quietly. "Before Mark gets too tired."

Kitty turned back to Mark and he clasped her

hand. It was the first physical contact between them. "Think about staying," he said urgently. "You ought to learn something about the ranch anyway. One day it'll be yours. Josh can explain things to you—about the ranch, about my other business matters."

Mark looked so tired that Kitty hated to argue with him, but she couldn't let him dwell in his fantasy. "I don't want anything from you, Mark, so don't trouble yourself doing the fatherly thing and leaving me a place I don't want. Anyway, that day's a long, long way off, so there's no sense even thinking about it now. I can only stay here until you're on the mend. I have a job to get back to, you know."

Mark released her hand. "We'll discuss it later," he said wearily. "Right now I want to rest."

Kitty nodded. "I'll come back to see you this afternoon." She moved toward the door, but Mark's voice stopped her.

"Kitten?" When she turned, he said, "I'm very glad you're here."

Kitty nodded again and, not trusting herself to speak, left the room.

Josh did not immediately follow Kitty out of the room because Mark said softly, "Stay a minute."

Josh looked down at his friend critically. "You look worn out, Mark. You really do need to rest."

Mark ignored the warning. "My daughter's really something . . . beautiful, classy, smart too. And independent as they come."

Josh silently agreed to everything Mark said,

but bit back his own mental list of her attri-
butes: sensual, alluring, argumentative, obstinate, hard.

Weak and ill as he was, Mark went on as
though he couldn't quit talking now that he'd
seen his only child after so many years. "She's a
lot like her mother, you know. The worst mistake I ever made was to let Jeanne and our baby
out of my life."

Josh knew he shouldn't encourage Mark to
keep talking, but he couldn't help but ask, "Why
did you?"

Mark grimaced. "Because I was a young fool
at the time, on an ego trip. Idiot that I was, I
believed my own image as one of the screen's
greatest lovers. It just didn't seem exciting to do
the domestic bit and go home every night to a
wife and baby. So I lost them," he ended heavily.
He pointed toward the window ledge. "There's
some paper and a pen over there. Bring them to
me."

Josh did as he was told, and while he held the
clipboard steady, Mark scrawled a few words on
the page.

"Take this to the bank," he told Josh. "I want
to open up a checking account in Kitty's name.
She'll need money while she's here, whether it's
only for a couple of weeks or for six months. I
don't want her to feel hampered in any way."

When Josh looked down at the paper and saw
the deposit amount, he couldn't restrain himself
from saying dryly, "It's not likely she'll feel too
hampered with this amount." He thought Mark
was being far too generous to a daughter who

hadn't wanted to see him in the first place, but
naturally he couldn't say so.

"I want you to take Kitty to the ranch tonight,"
Mark went on. "I want her to spend a little time
there, at least. Who knows? Maybe a miracle
will happen and she'll fall in love with the place
and want to stay."

Josh didn't like this idea at all. Mark still
wasn't out of the woods as far as his lungs were
concerned, and Josh thought his daughter ought
to remain near the hospital. He had no idea how
Kitty would feel about it, but he had a hunch
that for once they would probably be in accord.
He kept his thoughts to himself, however, and
said mildly, "We'll see. Right now you need to
get a nap. We'll be back to see you late this
afternoon after you've had a good rest."

Kitty waited for Josh in the downstairs lobby.
She sat stiffly upright in a vinyl chair and
watched other hospital visitors come and go.
God, what dreadful places hospitals were, she
thought. They seemed such impersonal, businesslike institutions, while all the time life and
death hung in the balance and human emotions
were played out in dramatic fashion. She saw
one group of people walk by supporting a dis-
traught woman. It would have been clear to
even the most dense observer that she had
either just lost a loved one or feared it was
imminent; at the same time, another cluster of
people seated nearby were laughing and congratulating a happy young man who had just
become a new father. In between the two ex-

tremes were all the other stories of sick or
injured patients, of fears and hopes and regrets.
Kitty felt like an interloper, viewing the private
emotions of strangers.

Was she like them? Could others read what
she was feeling, too? Yet she honestly wasn't
sure herself just what she did feel now that she'd
seen Mark. Actually, she was trying not to feel,
not to think. She'd come prepared to hate him, or
at the very least to be indifferent to him. But
now . . .

She was aware that someone had taken the
chair beside her. Her thoughts interrupted, she
glanced up to see Josh. "Well," he said as he
stretched out his long legs in front of him, "what
do you think of Mark now that you've seen him?"

Kitty's gaze followed the length of Josh's legs
and she fixed it on the tip of one of his boots.
"He's not the handsome lover he used to be on
the screen, is he?" Her voice was wry and
slightly unsteady. "He's not at all the same
Mark Winters who was once adored by half the
women in the country. Now he's got a receding
hairline, wrinkles on his face and hands, and he
doesn't appear to have quite the same strong,
husky build he once did." Her laughter was
brittle, a shield for how upset and worried she
really was. "If those women could only see their
idol now!"

Josh let out an angry breath between his teeth,
and his words, when they came, were scorching.
"That's about the sort of comment I'd expect out
of a woman like you. You think more of a person's looks than his character."

"Is that so?" Josh's anger instantly kindled hers. "So far in my life, I've met few men whose characters were worthy of admiration. My stepfather happens to be one of the few. As for Mark, his character has never been much to brag about. 'Pleasure before duty' has always been his motto!"

"With a daughter like you, maybe it's a blessing he took his pleasure elsewhere," Josh threw back.

Kitty felt as though she'd just been slapped. Unconsciously, she recoiled, closing her eyes for a brief instant to stop the sudden sensation of dizziness. When she opened them again, she got to her feet without a word and sped down the wide corridor and through the large glass doors.

The day was cold in spite of the bright sunshine, but Kitty was even colder on the inside. She felt frozen and numb and knew it was best to be that way, best not to feel. It was bad enough to let thoughts of her father throw her off-balance; she simply had no emotional reserves left with which to deal with Josh's attacks.

But suddenly a volcano erupted inside her, burning her with the hot lava of emotions long suppressed. Her eyes stung with salty tears, but she fought to hold them back. Her throat ached and she had an inner tremor that was frighteningly intense. Desperate to get away before she broke altogether, she stumbled blindly toward the street.

It had been traumatic meeting Mark after all this time. She hadn't expected to feel such pain at seeing the pitiful shadow of the vigorous man he'd once been. She'd had to control the urge to throw her arms around him, to call him Daddy, to say she loved him, to beg him to love her, to beg him to live.

Two powerful arms wrapped themselves around her waist, halting her aimless flight.

"I'm sorry," Josh murmured near her ear. "I was off base saying such things to you. Even Mark acknowledged to me that he hadn't been a father to you. Come on," he added gently as he turned her around to face him and captured both her hands, "let's get in the truck. You're chilled." Meekly, Kitty allowed herself to be led.

Josh felt like kicking himself as they crossed the parking lot. When he'd flung those last hateful words at her in the lobby, she'd gone so pale that for an instant he'd thought she was actually going to faint. But then she had gotten up with that blank expression on her face, as though she didn't even remember where she was, and started rushing toward the doors. The poor girl had been through a very difficult time ever since he'd first approached her with the news that Mark was injured. Today had been harder still. She'd had to see how ill her father was at this, their first meeting in over twenty years. All that would be hard enough on anyone, even without a jerk like himself recklessly tossing around insults and making things worse.

Once they were inside the cab of the truck, Kitty slumped forward, elbows on her knees, and buried her face in her hands in a gesture of absolute despair. Josh inserted the key into the ignition, trying to brace himself against the effect she was having on him.

It didn't work. A second later he muttered a curse and did the only thing it seemed possible to do. He pried her hands away from her face, pulled her into his arms and smothered her face with kisses.

At first Kitty was stiff, resisting him. Josh could feel the rigidness in her bearing, the tension emanating from within her, and that only incited him more. He crushed her tighter against him and his lips bruised hers with a hungering intensity that both amazed and appalled him.

And then Kitty responded. He felt it first in the released tension of her shoulders. His hands went up to stroke them, to caress the back of her neck. Kitty's hands slid around his waist and she clung to him as her soft lips parted beneath his. Her reaction inflamed Josh and wreaked havoc within him. An aching need spread through him, and he held her closer and closer until he could feel the warmth of her even through her clothing, until he could infuse her in turn with his own warmth.

But at last the intensity of the kiss they shared became gentler, softer, sweeter, though no less desirable. Josh's hands moved down from Kitty's shoulders to her back, along her hips, and back again to rest in the curve of her incredibly small waist.

The kiss ended and for a moment their warm, erratic breathing mingled before Josh pressed his cheek to hers. He felt Kitty tremble against him, and suddenly he wanted her so badly he was suffering the tortures of the damned.

"Why," he demanded gruffly, angrily, "did you have to come along and disturb my life?"

Swiftly, Kitty pushed him away. Her lips were unsteady, and in her eyes Josh recognized the same confused frustration and misery he was feeling.

"*You* barged into *my* life, not the other way around, remember?" she told him. Her voice was cold and distant, shutting him out with willful determination. "I don't want to disturb your life any more than I want my own messed up. Maybe," she added frostily as she turned her head toward the window, "you should just drive us back to the hotel. After that, you can go away and do whatever it is you normally do. I can take taxis to visit Mark at the hospital until it's time for me to go home again."

The frigid chill in her voice grated on him. "That's what you want?"

Kitty refused to look at him. "Yes," she answered tightly. "That's what I want."

"Lady, you've got it!" Josh strained to keep his own emotions under wraps as he started the truck, turned it into the street and took off as though high were the only speed he knew.

Chapter Four

"Mark, how many times do I have to say it?" Kitty sighed in exasperation. "I'm not going to the ranch. I came to see you, not a place in the middle of nowhere that's three hours away from you. Be reasonable. Crown, please," she chortled gleefully.

"I'm not unreasonable," Mark declared. "You are. I talked to Ellie last night. She's going to have my housekeeper get things ready for you, and Josh is coming for you today. I don't like you staying alone at a hotel. You'll be safer at the ranch. Besides, I really need you there to keep an eye on things for me." He placed a red crown on her checker, then jumped three of her men. "Now you crown me," he said smugly.

Kitty frowned over the loss of three of her men and returned to the subject at hand. "You've got two ranch hands, a part-time housekeeper, your friend Ellie and Josh besides, all there to look after things for you. You never needed me before and I'm not buying such a fairy tale now." She jumped Mark's last two men and gloated, "I win."

"You're a hard, unfeeling woman, Katherine Winters Peterson," Mark said, "and I know those traits didn't come from your mother. Or from me, for that matter."

"Hmmmph! Maybe not from Mom," Kitty allowed, "but we both know you're no saint." A teasing grin took the sting out of her words. "Which are you grumbling about, anyway—the fact that I won't go to your ranch to vegetate or because I just beat the pants off you at checkers?"

Mark's grin was rueful. "You can't beat my pants off because they won't let me wear anything except this hideously indecent hospital gown."

Kitty chuckled. "Well, you do look cute in it. I saw the way that new nurse was looking at you this morning. She thought she'd died and gone to heaven to be in here taking care of such a famous movie heartthrob."

"Cut it out!" Mark grumbled. "I'm too damned old to have to put up with star-struck imbeciles babbling about how wonderful I was twenty years ago."

"Crotchety, crotchety," Kitty gibed. "I do believe you really are a lot better, Mark. Acting like an old grouch is a sign you're getting well."

The medical news was encouraging. During

the past two days Kitty had had the opportunity to meet Mark's doctors. At first they had been cautious in their predictions even though Mark had weathered that one really awful night before Kitty arrived, but now their words were much more upbeat. It would still be a while before Mark could be released from the hospital, but it was clear that they no longer felt his life was in danger.

Kitty was far from feeling close to Mark, though she'd spent most of her time with him these past two days. All the same, they were slowly getting acquainted with each other, and if Kitty were strictly honest with herself, she'd be forced to admit she was enjoying his company as much as he seemed to be enjoying hers. True, they were both still wary and careful with each other. There were no references to the touchy subject of their estrangement, no accusations and no apologies concerning the past. It was as though they had an unspoken pact to leave the past to itself for the time being while they worked through the precarious present.

They'd been doing fine until this morning, when Mark had started badgering her again about going to his ranch near Brownwood. For some reason Kitty couldn't understand, it seemed to matter a lot to Mark that she spend some time there. For her part, she might not have been so vehemently opposed to it if the deal hadn't included Josh.

After that day in the truck, Josh had taken her literally and gone away. Fortunately Mark had not been suspicious about it because Josh told him he'd needed to go to Houston on business. But now he was coming back—at Mark's insistence—to take her to the ranch.

A nurse's aide entered the room carrying a lunch tray. Kitty, sitting on the edge of Mark's bed, got hastily to her feet and swept the checkerboard and checkers out of the way.

"I think I'll go downstairs to the coffee shop and grab a bite of lunch myself," she told Mark. "Do you want me to get anything for you before I come back . . . a newspaper or a magazine?"

Mark shook his head. "I don't need anything."

"I'll see you in about an hour, then."

Downstairs, Kitty bought a sandwich and an iced tea. When she turned to find a table, she saw Josh coming through the door.

He saw her at once and, detouring from the direction of the serving counter, came toward her.

For a time, they stared at each other somberly, both recalling the cold parting in the elevator at the hotel several days ago. Kitty caught her breath as, suddenly, he smiled at her.

She smiled back. She couldn't help herself. She shouldn't be glad to see him, but she was. Her eyes drank in the compelling sight of him, his height, the warmth in his gray eyes, the infectious magnetism of his smile.

"Hi," he said simply.

"Hi, yourself," she answered.

Josh gazed with appreciation at her fresh beauty, her dark, sparkling eyes, the wonderful smile she bestowed on him, and was amazed at how pleased he was to see her. He'd been dreading the encounter ever since Mark had asked him to come back from Houston and drive her to the ranch. Now all his resistance drained away.

All at once he became aware that she still held her tray. "Here, let me help you with that."

Kitty released it and followed Josh to a nearby table.

"How's Mark?" he asked as he straightened and looked at her once more.

"You haven't been up to see him yet?"

Josh shook his head. "I just arrived and decided to grab some lunch first. He sounds a lot stronger on the phone."

"He is a lot stronger, and the doctors are making encouraging sounds. The two of us had a fierce checker game this morning."

Josh grinned. "He must be doing all right, then." He removed his heavy tan coat and draped it over the back of the chair opposite Kitty's. "I'll be back in a minute, after I get my food."

Kitty watched as he went through the serving line. He wore dark brown slacks and a creamy beige long-sleeved shirt open at the throat. He was by far the best-looking man in the coffee shop, and she saw that she wasn't the only woman aware of it. A young woman in line ahead of him was initiating a conversation with him.

Kitty poured sugar into her tea, wishing she could be indifferent to Josh. She had meant what she'd said that morning in the truck. She didn't want to mess up her life with romantic complications any more than he apparently did.

She enjoyed having the companionship of men on occasion and rarely turned down a date with a likable one, but ever since Bob her heart had been carefully insulated. An occasional pleasant evening with a man was one thing; becoming emotionally involved was quite another.

For some reason Josh affected her in a way that other men did not. She was attracted to him physically—she might as well admit it—but there was more to it than that. Somehow she knew that there were depths to Joshua Steele that most men of her acquaintance didn't have. He might quarrel and disagree with her about certain things, especially the subject of Mark, but at least he was genuine. There was nothing fake about him.

Josh returned to the table with a barbecued burger, a slice of pecan pie and a cup of coffee. While he settled into his chair, Kitty asked politely, "Did you accomplish all your business in Houston?"

He paused in the process of unwrapping his burger to look at her. "Want the truth?"

"Of course."

"I could have taken care of it just as well with a ten-minute telephone call. I only went to get away from you."

"Well, thanks," she said slowly, feeling unaccountably hurt. She lowered her gaze to her suddenly unappetizing sandwich.

Josh had carefully noted her reaction to his words and his heart gave a little leap. He was, all at once, ridiculously happy. He reached across the table and covered Kitty's hand with his. She looked up, her brown eyes questioning, and he said very softly, "I told you the other day you disturbed me, but I found out I was more disturbed when I was away from you. I don't know why—and I don't like it—but I'm very attracted to you, Kitty, and that's the truth."

The pain that had lodged in Kitty's chest dissolved as though it had been no more substantial than a soap bubble. "Why," she asked from a dry throat, "don't you like it?"

Josh removed his hand from hers and shrugged. "There are a lot of reasons. For one, you're my good friend's daughter, and I'd hate to do anything that might jeopardize that friendship. For another, we might as well come from two different planets, for all we have in common. You're a city girl; I'm at my best where I can forget the rest of civilization even exists. And last, you're only here for a couple of weeks at most, so I don't see much point in starting anything we can't finish, do you?"

Kitty shook her head. "No," she said. "I don't. I . . . I agree completely with everything you've said."

"Everything?" A teasing glint came to lurk in Josh's eyes.

He was referring to what he'd said about being attracted to her—she knew that. Now he was probing her feelings, and because he'd just been honest, Kitty was in no mood to prevaricate either. She smiled and nodded. "Everything," she said firmly.

Josh appeared pleasantly surprised that she'd been so up-front about her own feelings. His eyebrows rose and he tilted his head. "Hmm-mmm," he said thoughtfully. "Now, that's very interesting. In that case, maybe we should reconsider our conclusion?"

Kitty relaxed and grinned. "No, indeed. It's by far the best solution. As you said, I won't be here very long. But it would be nice to know I could count on you as my friend while I'm here."

Josh's eyes narrowed. "Can we?" he asked. "Be friends, I mean? I wonder." He shook his head in a dismissing manner.

For a little while, they ate in silence. Then Josh asked, "Are you really going out to stay at the ranch? When Mark asked me to come for you, I wasn't sure whether it was wishful thinking on his part or whether you really wanted to go."

"It's wishful thinking on his part," Kitty admitted. "I think I ought to stay right here. After all, I came to see Mark, not the ranch. But he's so insistent about it and I don't understand why."

Josh frowned. "Maybe I'm telling tales out of school here, but you are his daughter and I think you ought to know. Mark has a bit of a heart condition." At the sudden alarm in Kitty's eyes he hastened to add, "Oh, it's not really too serious—so far, at least. He takes medication, which seems to be controlling the problem, but it's got him thinking about the fact that he's not immortal, that there is a limit given to any one man to live, and that perhaps it's time to mend his fences with you before anything happens to him. I think that's what prompted him to invite you to come out a few months ago. He was really devastated when you refused."

"I wish I'd known," Kitty said quietly. She thought of all the letters she'd returned unopened since her high school graduation, the unlisted telephone number taken specifically so that Mark couldn't phone her. When the invitation had arrived a few months ago, it had come through a letter to Jeanne. By then Mark had known that otherwise it wouldn't be read. But Jeanne hadn't known about Mark's heart condition either, Kitty was certain, or she would have pressed her to accept the invitation more urgently than she had.

"Anyway," Josh went on, "he's mentioned several times how everything he has will one day belong to you and that you ought to see the ranch. You were asking me the other day if I didn't mind my father selling our ranch to Mark. If it had to be sold, he was the perfect person for it. You see, that land used to belong to your great-grandfather and your great-great-grandfather before that."

"It did?" Kitty looked at him with fresh interest.

Josh nodded. "Mark's mother sold it to my father. Don't you know anything about your family background?" he asked with curiosity.

Kitty shook her head. "How could I? I didn't even know Mark, and my mother never told me anything about my father's family."

"Maybe that's what Mark wants you to learn," Josh suggested softly. "That it's not just a piece of land. That it's your roots."

Kitty nodded. "That must be it. I wonder why he didn't tell me."

"Possibly because he was afraid you'd reject your heritage the same way you rejected him."

Kitty glared at him. The warmth she'd been feeling since Josh arrived suddenly vanished. "I only rejected Mark after he'd rejected me one time too many," she said coldly. "And I'd very much appreciate it if you'd mind your own business."

Josh annoyed her further by seeming unperturbed by her outburst. "Suit yourself," he said with a shrug.

The long drive from Dallas to the ranch was accomplished later that afternoon. Kitty stared out the window of the pickup, watching the bright sun become increasingly covered with gray clouds as a cold front moved in.

The country became rocky, rolling hills and, to Kitty's city-bred eyes, bleak and lonely beneath the cold winter sky. This was the country Mark and Josh were so mad about? she wondered incredulously. True, it had a certain strength and grandeur, a permanence that was timeless, a vastness that was awesome; but to someone from her background, the wide open spaces seemed too spacious. The endless, unpeopled vistas, though they had a certain undeniable beauty, were lonely and melancholy. How could anybody love such an untamed environment?

They had passed the time during the drive by keeping up a steady stream of conversation.

They were determined to put behind them, at least for the time being, their friction as well as their keen physical awareness of each other. It was the only way to get through such a long confinement together.

"Do you have any brothers or sisters living near you?" Kitty asked idly.

Josh shook his head. "No, I was an only child."

"It seems to me," Kitty said thoughtfully, looking out the window at some grazing sheep, "that this must be a terribly lonely place to grow up."

Josh shrugged. "When you're born to it, you don't know anything different. The animals, the land itself are your friends. Besides, my best buddy lived only a couple of miles down the road. Still does, as a matter of fact, so I always had somebody to hang around with when I wanted company. I suppose the only time in my life I actually felt lonely was right after my mother died. I was fourteen."

"That must have been tough," Kitty said softly. "And your father?"

She saw a slight tension come to his jaw. "He died when I was twenty-two," he replied after a small hesitation, "but he'd been gone from the ranch since I was seventeen, so I was used to being on my own by then."

"Even so, it must have been hard, losing both your parents at such a young age. I guess in a way I can understand your fondness for Mark if he was so good to you."

Josh nodded, but kept his eyes on the downhill slope of the highway. "Mark wasn't around too often at first, but whenever he was, he did sort of take me under his wing. He taught me a lot about business and finance, gave me advice." He smiled whimsically. "And he even chewed me out a few times whenever he thought I needed that, too."

Kitty smiled back. "That's sort of how my stepfather's been to me," Kitty said. "He's only been in the family a couple of years and I'd already been living on my own for several years, but all the same I know I can count on him if I need help or advice. But the main reason I'm fond of him is because he's so good to my mother. It's nice to see her so happy and confident. She knows that he loves her, that no matter what, he'll come home to her every night."

Josh shot her a quick, inquiring look. "Didn't Mark?"

"Are you kidding?" Kitty retorted. "Didn't you ever read any of the gossip about Mark Winters? He openly cheated on my mother; on his second wife, too, I understand. It was common knowledge."

Josh shook his head. "I guess I was always too busy with my own life to pay any attention to things like Hollywood gossip. I hardly ever went to the movies, much less knew anything about the private lives of the actors. What seems strange to me is that in all the years I've known Mark, he's never seemed anything like you describe. He's always been steady and dependable. Why, when he finally decided to make the ranch his permanent home, his last wife was the one to walk out on him, not the other way around."

Kitty could tell by the tone of his voice that

Josh hadn't thought much of Mark's last wife, the one called . . . what was her name? She couldn't even remember. Long ago Mark's wives and numerous love affairs had ceased to hold much interest for her.

Still, she was a bit curious about this Ellie whom Josh and Mark both had mentioned. She said, "Tell me something about Ellie. Are she and Mark involved?"

"Ellie? She's one of the finest ladies west of the Mississippi," he answered with unmistakable sincerity. "She's been widowed about ten years, and though she still lives on her ranch, her son Adam runs it now. Adam's that best friend I mentioned before. We grew up together, and after my mother died, I guess you could say Ellie became my second mother." Josh shrugged. "As to whether there's anything going on between her and Mark, I really can't say. To tell you the truth, I never gave it any thought, though they have been good friends for years."

They drove through the town of Comanche, named after the Indian tribe, and beyond it past a number of peanut farms. Some thirty miles west, just at dusk, they entered the small town of Rising Star.

"It's not much further," Josh told her. He pointed out a modern bank as they passed through town. "We do most of our business either here or in Cross Plains up the road," he explained. "It's thirty miles to Brownwood from the ranch, so we generally go there only when we can't find something locally."

"Why isn't Mark in the hospital there?" Kitty

asked as they sped past a truck stop. "He'd be so much closer to home."

"He was, at first, but when he developed the lung problem, they airlifted him to Dallas where a team of specialists could care for him. One of the doctors there is a close friend of his, and Mark wanted to be under his care. Look!" he exclaimed, slowing the truck and pointing.

Just ahead, standing in the middle of the highway, were a doe and her fawn. Kitty caught her breath and watched, entranced, as the doe glanced toward them, for one brief moment seemingly mesmerized by the beam of the headlights. Then the pair turned and bounded away, vanishing into the trees.

"Beautiful!" she breathed.

Josh nodded. "If you'll notice, there are a lot of warning signs out here about deer crossings. It's easy to hit one at night if you aren't alert."

The truck crested a hill, and they turned off the highway onto a blacktopped rural road just as the last remnants of daylight vanished. Kitty was disappointed that her first visit to Mark's ranch should be in total darkness, but she contented herself with the knowledge that tomorrow she would be able to explore.

When Josh drove through a private gate, the headlights picked out a sprawling, modern brick house. A second truck stood in the driveway and two men lounged against it.

"Those are Mark's ranch hands," Josh told Kitty.

They got out of the truck and Josh introduced them. Red was a large redheaded man of about fifty, with a porky build and a guileless, ready smile. Oakie, who looked a little older, was tall and spare, with thinning hair and no smile at all, yet there was a likable gentleness in his blue eyes.

"Glad to meet you," Red said affably. "How long are you staying?"

"Just a week or two," Kitty replied.

"Anything you need while you're here, anything at all, jest let us know," Oakie told her. "You'll find our phone numbers on a bulletin board beside the kitchen telephone."

"Thanks." Kitty realized the offer was genuine, and she appreciated it.

"How's Mark doing?" Red asked.

For the next few minutes they discussed Mark's condition. When Josh unloaded Kitty's bags, the other two men said their goodbyes and took their leave.

Josh produced a key to the house. Inside, Kitty had a hurried glimpse of a spacious living room with a stone fireplace at one end before she followed Josh to a guest bedroom, where he deposited her luggage.

When Josh turned, he saw the forlorn expression on her face as she stood in the doorway. She looked sad, confused, out of her element, and he supposed she was. This was a long way from the busy thoroughfares of Chicago. Suddenly, he hated to leave her.

He strode across the room to her, but, recalling his resolve just in time, he didn't touch her.

For what seemed like ages, they gazed at each other, and the sexual tension they'd tried so hard to suppress during those hours together in the pickup abruptly flared to life again. Josh's eyes went again and again to the pink lips that looked so vulnerable and so infinitely desirable. Kitty was all wrong for him; she was light-years away from being the sort of woman who could fit into his life in any meaningful way. Yet his heart kept forgetting that fact. He kept forgetting their quick-tempered arguments, her unnaturally harsh judgment of her father, everything except how beautiful she was, how he sensed a softness beneath the granite, and how very much he wanted her.

"I'd better go," he said at last in a voice that sounded like gravel.

"Yes." Kitty's gaze clung to his. "I suppose you'd better."

"Are you afraid?" he asked after a moment. "To stay here alone?"

Kitty shook her head. "No. It just feels a little strange to be staying alone in a house that doesn't belong to me, that's all. I feel like an intruder."

She fought a sudden urge to reach out to Josh. She didn't want him to leave, and what she saw in his eyes made her quiver with unexpected yearning. If either of them took that single remaining step, they would be in each other's arms. Yet she didn't dare make that step.

"You could," Josh said gruffly, "come home with me."

He hadn't meant to say it, but the words just came, and his heart had meant them. More than anything, he wanted to make love to Kitty. It made no sense that he should want this particular woman more than any other he'd ever known, but there it was. What was more, she knew it, too. He'd just laid himself wide open.

Her lips trembled and she actually seemed to sway toward him. But then Josh decided it must have been his imagination because she shook her head.

"It . . . wouldn't be wise," she said softly. "We both know what would happen if I did."

She was right, of course. It wasn't wise. But when you wanted someone as badly as he did Kitty, it was hard to remember to be wise. Still, Josh respected her decision. Even more, he respected her for being so honest. Kitty didn't play coy games; she didn't pretend she didn't want him, too. She acknowledged it right up front, and to Josh that was most astonishing in a world where people could play such cruel games. Kitty might be turning him down—that was her privilege. But she wasn't toying with him.

All the same he was deeply disappointed. He nodded and, trying to mask his true feelings, said briskly, "Come on, let me show you around the house before I go."

As Kitty preceded him down the hall, Josh sucked in a deep breath of frustration. He despised himself for wanting her. Hadn't one wrong woman in his life been enough?

Chapter Five

By daybreak, Kitty, wearing jeans and a thick brown sweater, was outdoors. The ground was white with early-morning frost and the air was crisp and colder than she'd expected. She rubbed her arms briskly, wishing she'd worn a jacket.

She circled the house, passing beneath the spreading branches of a pecan tree. Behind the house, some distance away, was a modern, galvanized metal barn, and nearer, a smaller metal building that appeared to be a storage shed. Abutting both sides of the yard were grazing pastures and beyond the barn were woodlands. Those woods, Mark had told her, were littered with Indian arrowheads and other remnants of their occupation of the area. At one time this part of Texas had been the western edge of the white man's civilization, where only the few dared to settle on the fringes of the vast Indian territory.

The sky was clear; later the sun would warm the day. There was an unhurried serenity about her surroundings. From nearby Kitty heard a bird call and another answer it, yet nothing else stirred. The wind lay still and the countryside was hushed, not yet awake to the new day. Something deep inside her soul responded to the peace that seemed to pervade every single thing, as though all of nature were content.

Kitty rounded the opposite side of the house and pulled open the garage door. Inside the garage were Mark's blue pickup and beige Cadillac. Mark had given her leave to use them both, but last night she and Josh had been unable to locate the keys. She checked, but the keys were not in the ignitions, either.

Kitty's stomach grumbled abruptly. Her exploratory walk and the cold air had given her an appetite. She returned to the house, and after a bit of rummaging through the kitchen cupboards and the refrigerator, she soon had her breakfast cooking.

She felt terrific this morning. Last night had been her first good night's sleep since she'd left Chicago. It was surprising since she'd lain awake a long time, huddled in a tight ball, trying to get warm while thoughts of Josh tormented and tantalized her. What would it have been like to be cozy and warm sharing his bed?

Shameless thoughts! Kitty was disgusted with

herself as she sat down to eat. Why couldn't she stop thinking about that man? For years she'd schooled herself to be unmoved emotionally by any man, no matter how sweet his words, no matter how charming, no matter how sexually appealing. She had become an expert at deflecting amorous intentions and at restraining her own naturally tempestuous needs. She'd made a solemn promise to herself long ago that never again would she play the fool for any man. Until now, it had been easy to adhere to her self-imposed rules, but somehow Josh had a way of making her forget the rules.

Still, she comforted herself as she spread jelly on a piece of toast, she *had* resisted him last night, difficult though it had been. She could be proud of that. And when she returned home, she would be gladder still that she'd had the strength of character necessary to withstand temptation. All she had to do was be vigilant against her capricious emotions for another week, two at the most. Then distance would intervene; once she was back home, her self-respect and integrity would be intact and she would forget the man with the gray eyes in short order. She would will it so, and Kitty had a very strong will.

Forcing herself to think of something else, Kitty studied the kitchen. Like the rest of the house, it was large and thoroughly modern. Josh had told her that, shortly after Mark bought the property, this house had been built to replace the older one in which his own family had lived. It should have been lovely with its dark-

paneled cabinets, a chopping block in the center
of the room and built-in appliances, but somehow it wasn't. It was clean and reasonably neat,
but it lacked luster and personality. The walls
were a boring off-white and the kitchen curtains
were an even duller sandy beige. Green canis-
ters were on one counter; a red bowl with plastic
fruit was on another, next to a cardboard box
filled with plastic storage containers. On a utility stand beside the refrigerator were boxes of
cereal and bottles of vitamins.

The entire house followed the pattern of the
kitchen—dull, characterless decor and a hodge-
podge clutter of items that should have been
stored out of sight in cupboards and closets. For
such a wonderful house—especially the living
room with its showpiece fireplace made of stone
and petrified wood—Kitty found the place somewhat depressing and uninviting.

Just as she finished eating and carried her
plate to the sink, the telephone rang.

It was Mark, sounding quite chipper. "I know
it's early, but I couldn't wait to call. Did I wake
you?"

"No. I've been up for ages."

"Well," he asked eagerly, like a small child
hoping for a wonderful birthday treat, "what do
you think?"

"Of what?" Kitty teased, pretending to be at a
loss.

"The house," Mark exclaimed impatiently.
"The ranch."

Kitty chuckled. "You don't have to shout. I
haven't had a chance yet to see the ranch,

although I did take a short excursion in the backyard this morning. The house, though, is very nice."

"Do you really like it?"

"Of course. Though it could," she added frankly, "use a little sprucing up. The wallpaper's peeling in the bathroom, and the living room carpet looks like it could use a good shampooing."

"I suppose. I'm afraid I never noticed." Mark sounded deflated and Kitty mentally kicked herself. She kept forgetting the man was ill and that her honesty should be tempered by that fact.

"Men never do," she said with an air of condescension. "You need a woman around the house, Mark. You ought to get married again."

Mark chuckled, his good humor restored. "You know, not once, when I got married, was I thinking of the woman's housekeeping abilities." Kitty laughed too, and he added, "Since I don't have a wife, I guess you'll just have to stick around and take care of your old man and the house, too."

"Nice try," Kitty said dryly. "But since you've done without me quite well all these years, I can't see myself falling for that line."

"It was worth a shot." Mark sounded unperturbed, and he adroitly changed the subject. "Have you met Oakie and Red?"

"Last night when we arrived. They send their regards. By the way, Mark, where are the keys to your car and truck? Josh and I couldn't find them."

"Should be in the top drawer of the nightstand

in my bedroom. Ah," he added in a different tone, "I'll have to hang up now. They've come to play Dracula and drain some more of my blood."

"Don't let them take it all," Kitty said with a laugh. "I'll call you tonight after I've seen the ranch, and give you my verdict."

"You'll love it," Mark declared. "So much that you won't be able to resist staying for good."

"For good?" Kitty sputtered. "What happened to a few months?"

Her father laughed again and, without replying, softly hung up on her.

While she still had the phone in her hand, Kitty decided it was as good a time as any to call her mother. She'd only spoken to her once since being there, the day she'd first seen Mark.

Jeanne's first questions concerned Mark's health. "He's so much better, he's picking on the nurses and quarreling with me," Kitty told her. "I'm at the ranch now because he simply wouldn't take no for an answer. He's also insisting I stay for a long visit and learn about the ranch and his business affairs."

"And are you?"

"Of course not! I don't feel I have any claim on Mark's property just because I happen to be his only child. Whatever he owns ought to go eventually to someone he genuinely cares about, and I never was in that category. Besides, my life's in Chicago, not out here where, for all I can tell, the major excitement of the day is if a car passes on the road in front of the gate."

Her mother laughed. "Surely it's not that bad! What about that good-looking young man, Joshua? I felt sure he would provide a bit of excitement for you."

"Joshua and I," Kitty said not quite truthfully, "barely tolerate each other. He feels sorry for Mark for having such a hard-boiled daughter as me."

"Hmmmm. Does Mark feel that way too?"

"I'm not sure," Kitty admitted. "We're both just sort of tiptoeing around each other like a couple of strangers forced into close contact. He doesn't know how to be my father any more than I know how to be his daughter, and after all these years I'm not so sure it's even important anymore. I'm humoring him a bit because he's ill, but I don't see any reason to prolong my stay."

"You're still your father's daughter, Kitty," Jeanne said. "It may have taken Mark a long time to remember that he's a parent, but you shouldn't be too hasty about writing him off."

"Are you suggesting I stay here for months on end?" Kitty asked incredulously. "Just to justify an inheritance?"

"Not at all," her mother replied calmly. "All I'm saying is that you ought to give some thought to the idea of spending some time with Mark so you can really get to know each other. You haven't been there long enough yet to know for sure how you really feel toward him. I'd hate for you to look back years from now and have any regrets—and I'm not talking about material things!"

It was easy enough for her mother to be so broad-minded, Kitty thought in pique after they'd ended the call. The years had dulled any bitterness she might have had toward Mark.

But Kitty was in a vastly different position. Children should never be rejected by their parents. She felt strongly about that. All those times Mark had been too busy to see her, he had proved by his very indifference that he had rejected her, and now a secret part of her was afraid to let down her guard. By giving in to his wishes and staying for a lengthy visit, she would be laying bare her vulnerability to him. She didn't think she could stand to have her father reject her a second time.

The same reasoning applied to Josh. Kitty was appalled at her strong attraction toward a man she'd met such a short time ago, but equally important was her deep-rooted fear of being hurt. Bob's infidelity had cut deep, wounding her pride and bruising her self-confidence. It had taken her a long time to get over the blow he had dealt, and she had sworn that no man would ever again have the power to inflict pain on her.

Not happy with the direction her thoughts had taken, Kitty chose the best antidote: action. She located a pad and pencil and methodically went through the cupboards and refrigerator, making a list of supplies to pick up at the supermarket. Maybe this afternoon she would drive into town.

She had surveyed about half the cupboards when the doorbell rang. As she left the kitchen and went through the living room, she wavered between hope and dread that it would be Josh.

Instead, a pleasant-looking woman in her early fifties stood at the door. She was dressed simply in a red sweater, well-faded denim jeans and a corduroy jacket. Her short hair was iron gray and becomingly wavy, and her hazel eyes sparked with energy and warmth. In her hands she carried a plate covered with aluminum foil.

Kitty guessed at once who her visitor must be, even before the woman smiled and said, "Hi, I'm Eleanor Robbins, the local welcoming committee."

Kitty smiled back. "I'm Kitty Peterson. Won't you come in, Mrs. Robbins?"

"Call me Ellie," the woman said easily as she stepped inside the entrance. She offered the plate to Kitty. "Coffee cake."

Kitty accepted it, murmuring appreciatively, "Thanks. It smells heavenly. I'll make some coffee to go with it."

Ellie followed Kitty toward the kitchen. "How was Mark when you left him yesterday? He sounds much better on the phone, but that could just be my imagination."

Kitty placed the cake on the table. "He really is better. Enough so that he kept on nagging at me until I agreed to come to the ranch."

Ellie grinned. "He can be persistent." She sat down while Kitty busied herself with the coffee. "I'm so glad you came, Kitty. It's high time you and Mark got together. I know you had to bend a lot to come to him after the sort of father he's been, but I admire you tremendously for taking that crucial first step."

Kitty looked at her in amazement. "How do you know what sort of father he was?"

"He told me." There was compassion in Ellie's

eyes. "I know about all the important occasions he promised he'd be with you but didn't show up; the letters dictated to secretaries; the too-few phone calls and too-large checks or extravagant gifts to assuage his guilt. Mark was really rotten to you, but believe me, Kitty, he's paid for it since."

Kitty shrugged. "Maybe. But it doesn't erase twenty-four years of indifference."

"I know that." Ellie's voice was gentle. "He knows it, too. But it's never too late to forgive . . . or to change. For a long time Mark has deeply regretted the way he behaved and has grieved over your estrangement. He truly wants to be a part of your life now. Can you forgive him enough to allow him a place in it?"

"I can't answer that," Kitty said slowly, "because I honestly don't know." All the same, Mark went up a notch in her esteem because he had given Ellie a truthful, unvarnished version of the past. She would have guessed he'd have kept quiet about something that cast him in a less than admirable light.

Ellie reached out to clasp Kitty's hand. "Nobody ever said it would be easy," she said. "But you're young and resilient and Mark is neither of those things anymore. You've been hurt by his neglect, but I suspect he hurt himself most of all because he lost out on the irreplaceable years you were growing up. The time has come to make a fresh start, and I sincerely hope you'll make the effort, my dear. If you don't, someday you'll be sorry, and by then it may be too late."

Kitty mustered a smile. "You sound exactly like my mother."

Ellie laughed softly. "Mother's have a union, didn't you know? I have a son of my own, and I'm even the proud grandmother of a two-year-old. Let me brag a little while you pour that coffee."

Kitty admired the subtle way the other woman changed the subject once she'd made her point. Over coffee and the delicious coffee cake, Ellie talked about her family. By the affectionate way she spoke of her daughter-in-law, Kitty could tell that the two of them were very close.

"I'll bring Carol over to meet you soon," Ellie promised. "When I told her you were here, she mentioned having you and Josh to dinner one evening."

"Josh?" The name electrified Kitty.

Ellie didn't seem to notice how Kitty had tensed at the name. "Josh and Adam are great friends," she explained. "They're almost like brothers."

"Yes. Josh told me . . . and also how good you were to him after his mother died."

Ellie sighed. "Well, somebody had to show that boy some love after Meg died. He was so young and he needed guidance. His father already had a drinking problem, you see, and Meg's death just compounded it. He let the ranch run down and Josh took on responsibilities that were far too heavy for such young shoulders. He worked like a Trojan trying to save the place, but he just couldn't. There wasn't enough money to keep it going and his father just plain didn't care anymore."

Kitty felt something soften inside of her. Now she better understood the tension and sadness in Josh whenever he'd spoken of his father. Strangely enough, both of them had suffered because of their fathers.

The sun was beginning to lower in the western sky late that afternoon when Josh reached the Winters house. He rang the doorbell and shuffled his feet restlessly as he waited.

It had been a long day, and Josh was tired and hungry. When it was clear that no one was in the house, he walked back toward his truck.

In a way, he felt relieved. The less he saw Kitty Peterson, the better off he was. Or so he tried to kid himself. The truth was, she was constantly at the back of his mind, no matter what he was doing.

His hand was on the handle of the cab when he heard a vehicle on the road. He looked in the direction of the sound and recognized Oakie's green truck.

A minute later it came to a halt behind Josh's. Kitty hopped out of the passenger side while Oakie got out a bit more slowly.

"How're you doing today, Josh?" Oakie asked.

"Can't complain," Josh replied laconically.

"You been showing Kitty the sights?"

"I guess you could call it that. She's been helping Red and me put out feed in the pasture." He smiled shyly at Kitty before adding, "She's a pretty good worker. We might make a rancher out of her in time."

"Is that so?" Josh murmured. He didn't attempt to hide his disbelief as he glanced toward Kitty.

There was a lively sparkle in her eyes, and her cheeks and nose were rosy from being outdoors. Her lithe body seemed to contain an explosive amount of energy. She seemed almost to be dancing as she shifted from one foot to the other, as though she had too much vitality to remain still.

Josh braced himself against the appeal of her. Somehow he just couldn't envision such a delicately feminine and sophisticated creature as Kitty traipsing around in a winter pasture, tossing hay to a herd of hungry cattle. He thought derisively that the experience must have been a lark for her, an amusing little episode she could use to entertain her friends when she got back home.

Kitty laughed softly at Oakie's comment and wrinkled her nose at him. "I wouldn't go so far as to say that," she told him, "but I loved every minute of it. I had no idea how great it can be working in air that doesn't have automobile fumes."

The normally dour Oakie summoned up yet another of his rare smiles. "See?" he challenged Josh. "When the land's in the blood, there's nothing you can do to get it out. When she gets back up there to that Chee-cargo," he drawled, "I bet you a hundred dollars she'll get to feelin' so hemmed in, she'll come runnin' back for good."

Boiling resentment filled Josh over the mutual admiration society Kitty and Oakie had going between them. A primitive instinct leaped in his blood, strongly urging him to smash his fist into the older man's face to eradicate that silly smile. He was so shocked at the violence of his feelings that he actually took a step backward, away from the other two, as a self-imposed precaution.

"She's a city girl first," he argued. "That's in her blood too. A woman who's used to bright lights isn't about to settle for a simple, quiet life out here. She'd go stir crazy in no time."

Kitty shot him a swift look of surprise. And why not? Josh thought in disgust. He was giving an importance to Oakie's teasing words that was entirely unwarranted. She probably couldn't help wondering why he was acting like a first-rate idiot! He was wondering that himself.

If Oakie noticed there was more heat behind Josh's words than the circumstances called for, he kept it hidden behind a poker face. He got back inside his truck and gunned the motor. "You mark my words," he said mildly. "This little gal's got more grit than you might expect." He tipped the brim of his hat in a gesture of goodbye, shifted gears, and the truck backed away.

While Kitty waved, an inner demon continued to bedevil Josh. "Well," he drawled, "it seems you made a conquest there . . . and Oakie's a tough nut to crack."

Kitty lowered her hand, and the smile she'd worn slowly faded as puzzlement flickered in her eyes. "You sound as though you resent that he likes me."

Josh laughed shortly, angry because she saw through him so easily, angrier still because he was foolish enough to actually be jealous of a die-hard old bachelor like Oakie. "That's ridiculous," he snapped.

"It certainly is," Kitty replied curtly. Abruptly, she left him and went toward the house. She was inserting the key into the lock when Josh followed a moment later, and her voice dripped with sarcasm as she asked, "Did you come by for any particular reason, or are you just here to favor me with your charming company?"

Josh clenched his teeth. "I came on business, or I certainly wouldn't be here wasting my time watching you practice *your* charms on a man old enough to be your father!"

Kitty looked startled and her eyes narrowed. "Now you really are being ridiculous. Oakie and Red were both very kind to me this afternoon, and I see no reason why I shouldn't be friendly to them. Anyway, I fail to see what business it is of yours." She flung the door open and went inside the house.

Josh entered close behind her. "You're right," he grated. "It's not a damned bit of my business. Except that Oakie is no match against the flirtations of a beautiful, sophisticated woman like you. I don't want you to make a fool of him."

Kitty swung around and her eyes glittered like ice. "That's disgusting! I don't play cheap little games, and I resent your insinuations!" Her gaze was scathing. "I don't know what sort of women you're used to, mister, but you're way off base about me and I'll thank you to keep your nasty opinions to yourself!"

They glared silently at one another, clearly at an impasse. The grandfather clock against the wall measured out the seconds as though each were a long epoch in the history of their stormy relationship. It seemed to Kitty that she'd always known Josh, always been irresistibly drawn to him, always been fighting with him . . . and against her own feelings for him. Had there ever been a time when she hadn't known the shape of his head, the firm cut of his jaw, that tiny white scar on his forehead just above the left eyebrow? Certainly she had always known that he was a man of strength and endurance, a man who could love a woman with tenderness but, if betrayed, could hate with a frightening intensity. How she knew these things she had no idea, but she knew all the same.

Josh broke the still silence by stepping toward her. His hand went to her shoulder, and there was contrition in his eyes where anger had been. "I'm sorry," he said stiffly, then paused. "I guess," he went on with the ghost of a smile, "I was convicting you of a crime someone else committed."

It was a telling comment, but Kitty didn't dare ask for a more elaborate explanation. It was enough to know that sometime, someplace, Josh, like her, had been badly hurt.

She nodded and said lightly, "Yes, you did. Without a fair trial."

He released her shoulders and Kitty, suddenly needing to put some space between them, moved toward the sofa. She shrugged off her jacket and dropped it there. With her equilibrium restored, she reminded him, "You said you came on business. What business?"

Josh seemed to relax too. The evening shadows in the room were darkening, playing patterns across his face as he reached beneath his coat into the breast pocket of his shirt. "I have to visit Mark tomorrow so he can sign some legal papers I picked up from his lawyer. I thought maybe you'd like to go along."

"I'd love it," Kitty responded. "I was planning to go anyway, but I was dreading the long drive by myself."

Josh smiled. "It's settled, then. We'll leave about eight." He drew something from his pocket and held it toward her. "By the way, I also came to give you this," he said.

Kitty's eyes widened, but she made no move to take it from him. She had recognized what it was—a checkbook. "I don't understand," she said quietly.

"Mark gave instructions to open a checking account for you. I did."

"Well, you can just close it again," she said flatly.

"Don't be silly. Mark wants you to have this money. You may as well take it."

Kitty clasped her hands behind her back. They

were trembling because suddenly she was blazingly furious. "It's just like Mark to think he can buy my affections now just like he used to buy off his guilt!"

Josh stared at her blankly, at first not understanding her outburst, but suddenly he too was angry. "He's only trying to be thoughtful and generous, but do you appreciate that?" he asked harshly. "For thanks, you accuse him of having underhanded motives!" He crossed the space between them, reached around her and grabbed one of her hands. He thrust the checkbook into it. "Mark's a lousy father, all right, wanting to see that his daughter is taken care of financially! Poor little Kitty . . . so very mistreated!" An ugly sneer twisted his lips. "It seems to me that if you hate him so much, you could have better revenge by running through his money, not rejecting it."

Kitty's voice shook with rage. "I don't need any more of Mark's extravagant, empty gestures, and I certainly don't intend to listen to your biased judgment of me!"

Wildly, she threw the checkbook at him. It hit the side of his jaw before falling to the floor with a dull thud. The gesture shocked them both, and for one split second they stood rigidly, paralyzed by the stunning action.

Then Josh's face darkened. His eyes glinted dangerously and his nostrils flared. Without warning, he seized her, imprisoning her in his arms. His lips were ruthless as he kissed her, and his embrace, when she tried to free herself, was punishing.

Kitty struggled but the kiss went on. His mouth was hard, bruising hers. Josh was heedless of her efforts to break the contact. The more she tried to resist, the more unyielding, the more ruthless and harsh he became.

Worse yet was the fire that ignited inside her, the ache of desire that spread through her limbs, perversely making her long to cease the struggle and give into the burning sensations that filled her with an urgent need that went quite beyond logic.

She fought her feelings even as she fought Josh, and when he pushed her from him at last, Kitty was as outraged with herself and her treacherous reactions as she was with him. He had dared to judge and criticize her, and worse still, he'd taken unpardonable liberties.

"You're nothing but a barbarian!" She lifted an unsteady hand to her swollen lips and ordered with as much force as she could summon, "Get out! Get out of here this minute! And keep away from me, do you hear?"

Josh's face, dark with his own violent emotions, went white; then a deep, angry red surged into it again.

"No woman," he said coldly, "orders me to do anything, and certainly not you." A malicious smile quirked the corners of his lips. "How misleading you are, with your pretty, feminine ways," he continued hatefully. "Yet for all that, all you really are is a coldhearted, militant female. You're exactly the type of woman I take pains to keep my distance from. You're worth-less to a man because you're all bound up in your hatreds and your prejudices and your struggle for power. You want me to stay away from you?" He presented a mock bow. "It's entirely my pleasure!"

Chapter Six

$\mathscr{K}$itty skipped visiting her father the next day.
She told herself it was because she was too busy
in her self-imposed task of housecleaning.
Mark's part-time housekeeper, Alma, was there,
and while she performed the regular chores,
Kitty decided it was a good time for her to tackle
the clutter. She found storage places for the
miscellany of things in the living room and
kitchen that so offended her sense of order, and
later she polished the kitchen cabinets. She
even found time to restore the luster of the brass
lamps and carved wood art objects in the living
room. By evening she was tired but pleasantly
satisfied with her efforts. She'd made a beginning.

The real reason she'd stayed home was that
she didn't want to chance meeting Josh at
Mark's bedside. After the hard words they'd

hurled at each other, it had been out of the question to keep their date to visit Mark together. And since Josh would still be making the trip to discuss business with Mark, it had seemed prudent to postpone her own visit by a day.

Kitty had been more wounded by Josh's harsh statements than she dared admit to herself, and because it hurt to think of him at all, she had found solace in the hectic activity of work.

The next day, however, as she made the long drive to Dallas in Mark's Cadillac, there was little to distract her and a strange ache came to her throat every time she thought of Josh. She tried to tell herself he simply didn't matter to her, but a small, insistent voice kept silently insisting otherwise.

When she arrived at Mark's hospital room, her low spirits lifted in spite of herself. Mark was positively beaming.

"Did you bring some champagne?" he demanded at once.

Kitty raised her eyebrows. "Was I supposed to?"

"Harvey," Mark said, referring to his doctor, "was just here." He paused dramatically before announcing, "He said I can probably go home this weekend."

"Fantastic!" Kitty was genuinely pleased for him. She sat down on the edge of the bed and clasped his hands. "The champagne will be chilled and ready when you get there."

"Fair enough." Mark grinned.

He did appear much improved, Kitty decided. His skin had taken on a touch of color and his eyes were deep blue, bright and alert. Compared to the pale, gray-faced, seriously ill man she'd found on her first visit, he looked magnificent.

"Ellie sends her love," she told him, counting off a finger. She raised a second one and added, "She also asked me to tell you someone named Ken from Abilene is interested in buying one of your bulls. He also passed along a message. Something about how he has a mean horse you might like to try to break since yours didn't finish you off."

Mark chuckled appreciatively. "That old son of a gun! I ought to tame that ornery stallion just to show him what a real man can do. He's sure not up to the job."

Kitty grinned too. Men, she mused, had a funny way of showing their affection for each other. The ruder the comments they made about each other, the better friends they usually were. "I spoke with Mom," she continued, raising a third finger, "and she sends her love too. She said she hopes your spirit hasn't been crushed by all this and that you aren't letting the nurses browbeat you into eating pudding."

Her father laughed heartily. "Imagine Jeanne remembering that all these years! I believe the first fight we ever had was over a pudding she'd made. She had no idea I hated it, and I'm afraid I wasn't very diplomatic. It wasn't funny at the time, but it became one of those stupid jokes between us that married people always have." He shook his head. "Tell her that despite the nurses' best efforts, I still haven't sunk that low."

"I will," Kitty said, grinning.

Abruptly, Mark became somber. "Tell her I appreciate her concern, too, Kitten. It's really decent of her."

Kitty nodded. "I'll do that. Now," she added sternly, "we'd better discuss that checking account you had set up for me. I can't accept it, Mark. In fact, I'm surprised you even thought I would."

Mark sighed. "Josh told me yesterday you'd refused it. Look, Kitten, you'll need money while you're here and—"

Kitty cut him off, shaking her head vigorously. "I won't be here that long. If you're coming home this weekend, I'll stay a couple of days more after that to visit with you, but then I'll have to get back to my job." When Mark looked as though he might protest, she went on more stridently. "I don't want your money, and I consider it an insult that you thought you could use it to bribe me into staying. You're just like Josh. You think I'm heartless and mercenary . . . that I'd try to take advantage of you."

"That's not true," Mark denied in a voice filled with agony. "My God, Kitten, you've rejected every gift I've sent since you were eighteen years old. Why would I believe you've softened now? I only thought that if you did decide to stay a few months, you'd need money to replace what you'd be earning at your job. Bills have a way of coming regularly and I just didn't want financial concerns to be the deciding factor about whether or not you stayed. Besides, even if you don't stay, this trip has cost you money. I'm grateful you came, but I don't want the expenses coming out of your pocket—especially when I can so easily afford it. As a favor to me," he pleaded, "accept the money."

Kitty shook her head, swung to her feet and began to pace the room. "Don't you understand?" she demanded hotly. "I don't want any part of your money. I can afford to take care of myself the short time I'm here, and I *will* be going home soon, Mark, make no mistake about it. You've got a romanticized fantasy that a few months together can make up for twenty-four years, but that's impossible. We've seen each other and at least we're back on speaking terms. It's too late for anything more, so let's leave it at that, shall we?"

Mark flinched at the uncompromising words and closed his eyes. When he opened them again he said in a wan voice, "I'm really tired. Maybe you'd better go now."

Kitty was unmoved. She glared at him and said sharply, "You're just putting on an act, hoping I'll drop the subject. Cut it out, Mark! This isn't a movie set!"

Mark's eyes widened and a slow grin spread across his lips. "How did you know?" he chuckled. He didn't seem at all annoyed that she'd seen through his ploy.

"I saw all your films," Kitty replied acerbically. "Numerous times. I may not know much about fathers, but I'm an expert on the subject of Mark Winters the actor. I can name every film, every Broadway play, even the years they were done. You were nominated for an Academy Award four times and you won one Oscar. You—"

"*Touché*," he interrupted softly. "I get the point." He looked wistful. "It's no use wishing you were an expert on fathers or that I were an expert on daughters, but can't we at least be friends?"

This time Kitty was moved. The appeal in his voice was earnest; no hint of acting colored it now. She remained stonily silent for a moment longer, but finally she nodded. "We can try," she whispered.

A slow smile relaxed Mark's face. "Okay, friend," he said, "tell me what's going on with you and Josh. You said he thinks you're mercenary and heartless. I had hoped you two would like each other."

"Not a chance!" Kitty began pacing again. "We rub each other the wrong way. He's too opinionated and judgmental."

To her amazement, Mark looked highly amused. "Seems to me the same things could be said of you. I suppose Josh would find you a bit difficult to understand, though. The sort of woman he'd get along with best is one who doesn't consider the entire male sex her natural enemy."

"And who's fault is that?" Kitty demanded bitterly. .

"I may be partially to blame," Mark said thoughtfully, "but your ex-husband must surely bear his share of it, too."

Kitty couldn't meet his eyes. She went to stare

out the window at the somber, gray day. "That's right," she said in a choking voice. "Bob was exactly like you. He thought himself God's gift to women. It didn't seem to occur to him to be faithful to his wife. The marriage vows he took were nothing but a joke."

"All right," Mark said gruffly. "I deserved that crack. But listen, Kitten, you've become too hard, too filled with hate. Did your mother turn into such a bitter woman, too?"

Kitty cringed at the unflattering description of her. Was she, she wondered bleakly, really like that? She turned toward him, surprised at both his question and her answer. "No," she said softly, "she never has seemed bitter, toward you or men in general. I guess she has a more forgiving nature than I do."

It wasn't pleasant to be confronted by her defects, but once raised, the subject nagged at Kitty like an unrelenting headache. That night as she undressed for bed, she caught sight of herself in the mirror and paused to study her reflection. Her long black hair billowed around her slender bare shoulders, her eyes were dark and thoughtful, and her mouth, dusky pink, appeared gentle and feminine. Was she really, she asked herself again, an implacable, forbidding man-hater? The idea was appalling.

But then she thought of Josh's kisses, of the fast-spreading heat aroused by his lips, by the touch of his hands, and the question was answered. She might have a strong resistance to becoming involved with a man, a fear of opening herself to possible pain, but emotionally, physically, she now saw that she had little strength at all. Josh had managed to storm her defenses and render them useless against her deep-rooted longing for a loving relationship.

Shivering, Kitty turned from the mirror. Her eyes were glazed as she looked across the bedroom but saw instead the empty years ahead. After Bob, she'd convinced herself that she could easily live without a man, without sex, without companionship and affection, without love. Meeting Josh had changed all that and brought her previous conviction to doubt.

Yet Josh despised her. It wasn't fair! It wasn't fair that he had awakened feelings within her that could never be appeased.

Despite the yellow rain slicker, Kitty felt the icy fingers of the rain poke through her clothes and attack her skin. Her feet were soaked and numb and the legs of her jeans were saturated with rain and mud.

"Okay," Red shouted, "easy does it. Now pull."

With all her strength, Kitty tugged at the heavy tree branch that Oakie and Red had attempted to dislodge from the brush. The heifer that had become entangled in it all lowed softly. It was as though she were trying to offer encouragement to the humans who were attempting to help her.

The unwieldy branch moved perhaps an inch, but that was all. "It's still hung up on something," Kitty yelled.

"Yeah, I see what the trouble is. Hold on and don't let go. Red, keep that brush lifted or it'll swing back and slap Kitty in the face."

Oakie waded into the tangled knot of vines and needle-sharp briars. He tugged and pulled and shoved and suddenly it was done. Kitty felt the branch work loose. She pulled with all her strength and it slid out of the snarled clump of thorny brush.

Freed, the heifer got to her feet. Both men stooped to run practiced hands over her limbs. Satisfied that she was all right, Oakie slapped her rump. The animal bellowed her gratitude and lumbered slowly away.

Despite the inclement weather, it had been a busy day for them all. Red had discovered a break in the fence that separated the north pasture from a neighbor's, and they'd spent the entire morning rounding up the half dozen cattle that had strayed through the opening. After that, of course, the fence had required immediate repairs. Then, to cap a miserable day, while closing one of the gates on their way out, Kitty had spotted the trapped heifer.

When they finally returned to the barn, it was past three in the afternoon. Now the rain chose to stop, though that offered little relief to the wet, bedraggled group. But they were grateful for what rain they'd had. The long drought of the past couple of years had badly hurt the ranchers, the men explained to Kitty, forcing many to sell off parts of their herds at a loss. Consequently, whatever rain they got was received with heart-felt gratitude. Today's, Oakie told her, had been a good one, more than an inch of slow, steady rain.

Inside the barn, Red checked the supply of grain that would be needed the next day, while Kitty located the first-aid box. Oakie had received a nasty scratch on his neck from the brambles when they'd rescued the heifer, and Kitty took some ointment and treated the wound.

With these matters attended to, they all went out once more into the raw, cold day. Kitty was startled to see Josh's truck pulling up beside Red's. Her heart started to race erratically as he got out and came toward them.

"I brought that pipe you said you needed," he said to the men.

"Good." Red went toward him. "We'll put it in the back of the truck now."

For only one brief instant, Josh's eyes rested on Kitty's face. They no longer contained the explosive anger she'd last seen in them. Now they were merely indifferent. Her heart sank as he nodded casually before turning to help the men unload his truck.

While they worked, the ranch hands favored Josh with an account of their difficult day. He listened with sympathy and then asked the question that was uppermost in his mind. "What's Kitty doing with you?" In the one glance he'd permitted himself, he'd noted her wet, muddied, disheveled appearance.

"She worked right with us all day," Red told him. "Wouldn't stay in the truck and keep dry like we tried to get her to do when it started raining."

"When we freed that heifer, it took three pairs of hands," Oakie added. "Don't know what we'd have done without her."

"That girl's not afraid of hard work or gettin' wet and dirty, that's for sure," Red said with low-voiced approval. Together they heaved the remaining pipe onto the bed of the truck. "Well, that's it. You ready to go, Oakie?"

"You bet." Oakie nodded at Josh and waved a hand toward Kitty, who had just closed and locked the barn door.

As the men drove away, Kitty set out walking across the soggy ground toward the house. Josh fell into step beside her. "You know," he observed conversationally, "even wet and muddy, you're still beautiful."

Kitty favored him with a skeptical frown. "Am I supposed to be flattered by that remark?"

"Maybe not flattered," Josh said, grinning, "but I'd hoped you'd be a little pleased. You're still mad at me, aren't you?"

She looked startled by the direct question, but her answer, another question, was equally direct. "Do you blame me?"

"No." Josh was no longer grinning. "I don't. I was pretty hateful," he admitted. "But so were you."

Kitty said nothing. They had reached the house, and she mounted the porch steps and opened the kitchen door.

Without waiting for an invitation that might

never be forthcoming, Josh followed her. Kitty paused to shed the rain slicker and her muddy shoes, and as he stood beside her, Josh immediately noticed the changes in the kitchen. Without the usual boxes and stacks of clutter, it looked more spacious and a lot cleaner. There was an inviting order and sparkle to the room that made it seem warm and cheerful.

"I always thought Mark managed pretty well with just the part-time housekeeper, but I can see you've made an enormous difference in here. It looks wonderful. I have to compliment you, Kitty, on what you've done—here in the house and out in the pastures, too. The men told me how hard you worked with them. I know Mark will be pleased."

"I didn't do any of it for your approval," Kitty snapped. Her eyes flashed fire. "Or for Mark's either, for that matter. Whatever I've done, I did it simply because it needed doing, not for any other reason."

Her angry retort, when he'd sincerely been complimenting a job well done, snapped Josh's self-restraint. In two steps he was beside her and his hands grasped her upper arms. He gave her a little shake and his voice was sharp with his own anger. "Why," he demanded, "are you always so quarrelsome, no matter what I say? All I did was try to say something kind, yet I got my head bitten off for my pains. I've never met a more difficult person in my life. Are you always this belligerent with everyone, or is it something about me that brings out the worst in you?"

Kitty stared at him for an eternity, it seemed.

Her lips parted as though she would speak, and yet she didn't for a time. Instead, she just looked at him, her dark eyes large as saucers in her pale face.

Then she completely disarmed him. Bowing her head slightly, she said in a near whisper, "I . . . apologize. I have been awful. I . . . I think you do bring out the worst in me. It's just . . . it's just . . ." Helplessly, her frail voice trailed away.

Josh groaned and drew her closer so that his arms could slide around to her back. "You're likely to drive me completely mad before too long," he muttered as he kissed the top of her head. He lifted one hand to smooth back the wet tendrils of her hair, and as he did, she raised her head. The uncertainty that was in her eyes echoed the same doubts in himself, and that only added to his undoing. He groaned again and bent lower to kiss her lips gently.

"I'm getting you wet," Kitty protested as he pulled her closer still and pressed her wet head to his chest.

"Hush," he told her as he stroked her head. "It doesn't matter. At least we're not fighting anymore."

Kitty laughed softly at that and Josh marveled at the loveliness of the sound. Why did they always seem to be fighting, he wondered, when it was so obvious that there was this strong, insistent attraction between them? It made no sense.

He became aware that Kitty was trembling. She was still wet and cold. Reluctantly, he released her, smiling down at her and noticing with satisfaction that a little color had surged to her cheeks.

"I'm an idiot," he said huskily, "keeping you standing here in those wet clothes. Tell you what—you go take a hot bath while I make some coffee. Unless," he couldn't resist suggesting, "you need help getting out of those soggy things?"

An even warmer glow stained her cheeks at his words. Then, with a very definite shake of her head, Kitty said firmly, "I can manage just fine by myself." But she was laughing when she said it.

"That's too bad," Josh answered, and this time he was no longer teasing. Even muddy and wet, with her hair plastered to her head and no trace of makeup on her face, he thought her the most desirable woman he'd ever met.

Kitty gazed at him for one long instant more before saying huskily, "I won't be long." She turned and hurried out of the room.

Left alone, Josh sucked in several deep breaths before busying himself with the prosaic chore of making coffee. He ached with frustration. All the same, he was glad Kitty had left him before things could get out of hand.

She was all wrong for him and he needed to keep reminding himself of that. Kitty was a city girl, and city girls needed a whirlwind social life, excitement and expensive baubles. As Mark's daughter and only heir, someday she would be a wealthy woman as well, putting just that much more distance between the realities of their lives. No, Kitty was out of his league altogether. He had nothing to offer someone like her, and if they made the mistake of becoming involved, it would only lead to complications. Complications, humiliation and pain, none of which he needed.

Josh strode to the window and gazed at the wet, forbidding afternoon. Moisture dripped from bare tree branches, and brown puddles dotted the yard. The sky was growing darker and heavier; it might still rain some more before the day was over.

His thoughts returned to the woman who, inexplicably, had cut through the barbed wire fence surrounding his heart. It did little good, he realized bleakly, to remind himself of all the reasons why he shouldn't—couldn't—have her. He just went right on wanting her.

Chapter Seven

Following Red's directions, Kitty drove toward Josh's ranch with a mingling of curiosity and trepidation. She had never seen Josh's home and couldn't help but wonder what it was like, but at the same time she was reluctant to see Josh himself.

When he kissed her the other day, she'd had a feeling they had reached a turning point. He'd been provocative and teasing, and when she'd gone away to bathe she had tingled with expectation. She would invite him to stay for dinner, and after that . . . Recklessly, she'd decided that she would stop fighting the attraction between them, that she would accept whatever the moment brought, grateful that—temporarily, at least—her loneliness was at an end.

But after she'd returned to the kitchen, Josh

had been different, restless and distant, as though he'd regretted the impulse of kissing her. By the time he had left, she'd felt nothing beyond the most extreme relief. If Red hadn't asked her to run this errand for him, she wouldn't now be turning through the gate onto Josh's property. She would never have had the courage.

Beyond the gate, a narrow wooden bridge spanned a dry creek. Kitty held her breath as the truck clattered across; she released it only when she was on solid ground once more. The road curved around a clump of pin oaks and then she saw the house.

Small and plain, the brown wooden structure had a stone chimney at one end. Two half-grown pear trees in the yard thrust their stark, winter-bare branches toward the brilliant afternoon sky. Off to one side was a small grove of peach trees.

On the other side of the house was a garage. Josh's truck was in the drive in front of it. Kitty parked behind it, and now she could see a barn farther back. In a nearby pasture a few Angus and Charolais placidly grazed.

Josh stepped out of his workshop behind the garage and saw Kitty walking toward the back of the truck. Her movements were purposeful and confident; abundant energy put a buoyant spring in her steps. Her unrestrained hair swayed against her royal blue sweater, while her hips, their delicate curves so beautifully displayed by a pair of beige jeans, swung gracefully with every step. For a timeless moment his heart stopped.

Two evenings ago, when she'd rejoined him
after her bath wearing a fleecy blue robe and a
matching ribbon threaded through the damp
curls of her hair, he'd been so shattered by the
intimate sight that it was all he could do to fight
the overwhelming urge to scoop her into his
arms and carry her off to the bedroom. He'd only
managed to avoid such a mad act by reminding
himself grimly of Dana. Fortunately, the trick
had worked. The recollection of his ex-fiancée,
and the ignominious end their relationship had
come to, was all he'd needed to help him put on
the brakes. The last thing he wanted in his life
was a repeat of that failure.

All the same, he couldn't help but be glad that,
for whatever reason, Kitty was there. He went
toward her.

"Hi. This is a nice surprise."

Kitty had lowered the tailgate. She lifted her
head at his greeting and her smile was so blind-
ingly lovely that Josh caught his breath. What
was it about her, he asked himself, that made
other women seem dull and lifeless by compari-
son? Surely there were others more appealing.
Kitty's chin was too resolute, her will too implacable, her resentments too glaring for him to be
seriously attracted to her. Surely. Yet the
warmth in her smile—whenever she forgot to be
defensive or angry—could have melted an ice-
cap; the perfect proportions of her slender body,
coupled with her soft white skin and her compel-
lingly beautiful eyes, tempted him almost beyond reason. Ironically, even her sharp, unsen-

timentalized outlook on life had a peculiar charm for him. Kitty didn't put on a false front of simpering femininity to hide an iron interior the way so many of her sex did. She was honest and forthcoming; you took her as you found her. And though they had clashed often, Josh found he admired her more than any other woman he'd ever met.

"Hi, yourself," Kitty said. "Red picked up your barbed wire in town and asked me to bring it over. He's helping Oakie put in a new water pump at his house."

"Thanks. If you'd called, I would have come by for it and saved you a trip."

"I didn't mind." Kitty's grin was infectious as she confessed, "Actually, I wanted to see your place, and this gave me a good excuse."

"You didn't need an excuse, you know," Josh said thickly.

A strange tension gripped them. They looked at each other for a long moment: something flickered in Kitty's eyes, but Josh wasn't sure what it was. And then she was speaking.

"It's very nice, Josh. I like it." She broke the contact of their eyes and glanced around.

"It's okay." Josh shrugged. "Nothing fancy like your father's place, but it suits me."

"I should think so!" Kitty declared emphatically. "Everything looks very new and neat," she observed.

"The house is about two years old," Josh said. "I lived in a secondhand trailer while I was building it." He squinted against the sun as he, too, surveyed the place. "I only finished the garage and workshop a few months ago." His gaze returned to her face. "Work goes slow when you can't afford to hire help and you're paying for every board and nail as you go along."

He carried the bundles of wire into the garage. When he came back, he shut the tailgate of the truck with a loud thud.

Kitty had recognized the defensiveness in his voice, as though he were daring her to compare his need for economy with Mark's affluence and perhaps pity him. Pretending she hadn't heard the strident note, she said, "The satisfaction of accomplishment must be enormous, not to mention the pleasure of knowing you don't have a lifetime of mortgage payments ahead of you. I envy you."

Her words won her a lukewarm smile. "There were times when I'd have been overjoyed if I could just wake up one morning and find the whole job finished. As for the mortgage, I have a large enough note on the land as it is without adding the price of a new home to it. Would you," he asked hesitantly, "like a tour?"

"I thought you'd never ask," Kitty laughed.

First Josh showed her his workshop, which Kitty quickly realized was his pride and joy. In the center of the shop was a beautifully constructed dining table that only needed staining and varnishing to be complete.

"You made this yourself?" she asked incredulously. The rounded base was exquisitely crafted, and Kitty stooped to run her hand over the silky-smooth wood. "This is really beautiful!" Admiration was evident in her voice. "You're a talented artisan."

He shrugged. "It's just a hobby."

"You could go into business if you wanted to."

Josh grinned and shook his head. "I'd have a problem there. I like to build what I want, not what someone else might want."

Kitty laughed and conceded, "That could be a problem, all right."

Next Josh showed her the barn.

"I understand the drought has been really tough on cattlemen the past couple of years," Kitty ventured.

"Devastating is more like it," Josh responded. "In the past year I've sold off about half my herd because I couldn't afford to keep feeding them. I'm just hoping I can hold on until things get better. If I didn't have an income from my job with Mark, I'd be in pretty dire straits."

"And then you'd have to make furniture to please other people, hmmmm?" Kitty teased. At once she became serious again. "It sounds as though ranching can be a precarious way to make a living."

"It is."

Kitty looked at him curiously. "But you'd never give it up," she stated with conviction.

A strange expression came to Josh's eyes, a sudden hardening, as though her words had brought back some unpleasant memory. "No," he said, his voice unexpectedly harsh, "not willingly. The only thing that would ever drive me away would be bankruptcy, and I intend to do my damnedest to keep that from happening. This place means more to me than expensive cars or fancy houses with swimming pools or European vacations."

"Hey! Hey!" Kitty exclaimed softly. "How did we get on the subject of swimming pools?"

The stern gray eyes slowly lost their belligerency. "Sorry," Josh muttered. "Come on. I'll show you the house now."

Kitty decided it was best to follow his lead and let the matter drop. They'd been enjoying themselves, and she didn't want any sour notes to spoil it.

They entered through the kitchen, and Kitty was immediately entranced. Lovely walnut cabinets contrasted with warm terra-cotta countertops, and the soft color was picked up again by the narrow blinds at the windows. The work area was efficiently arranged, and a long breakfast bar separated the kitchen from the living room.

The warm earth tones of the kitchen carried through to the living room, with its walnut paneling and a beautiful stone fireplace dominating the end wall. A stone planter set off a small area near the kitchen where the formal dining table would go.

The remainder of the house consisted of two bedrooms and a bath. The larger bedroom was Josh's, while the smaller one was used as an office. Josh explained that the house had been designed so that if additions were needed later, it would be an easy matter to do so without spoiling the look or the convenience of the original structure.

"You have a beautiful home, Josh," Kitty said as they returned to the living room. "I'm so impressed with all the work you've done—crafting your own furniture, the built-in bookcases and deep closets."

Josh shrugged, refusing to take the compliment seriously. "Mark's bedroom is larger than my living room. You can't be that impressed."

"No?" Kitty was suddenly annoyed by the way he kept comparing the classic simplicity of his home to the extravagant elegance of Mark's. "You wouldn't be so quick to put it down," she snapped, "if you could see my apartment. This house must be three times its size and ten times as convenient."

Josh appeared startled by her vehement indignation. There'd been a frozen look to his face, but suddenly it thawed. "I keep forgetting that you don't live like a rich man's daughter," he said softly.

Kitty sighed. "Believe me, I don't forget it for a minute. There've been occasions toward the end of the month when I've been reduced to eating soup and crackers."

Josh grinned. "So that's what maintains that luscious figure! And I thought it was those strenuous exercises you were doing the night I met you." His gaze was frankly admiring as it meandered down her body.

When his eyes returned to her face, they both

became solemn, riveted by a strong tension that was as tangible as the furnishings of the room.

Kitty's gaze went to the droop of Josh's hair across his brow. She felt a powerful urge to brush it back. She wanted to see his mouth soften, his face relax into a smile. She wanted to touch the broad shoulders, to be held close to the wide, firm chest. The desire shook her and she forced herself to look away. "I'd better go," she said unsteadily. "I'm keeping you from your work."

"Stay. Have dinner with me."

The insistence in his voice brought her gaze back to Josh's strangely rigid face. The tension was still between them. Kitty hesitated, trying to think of reasons why she should go . . . and failing.

"I'd like that," she found herself replying at last. "Very much."

Together they prepared a simple meal. Somehow the mundane business of broiling steaks and chopping salad freed them from the defensiveness and inhibitions that up until then had marred their times together. They laughed a lot and talked about anything that came into their heads.

Over dinner, Josh asked her about her marriage. "It was an utter flop from the beginning," Kitty said frankly. "I was young, naïve and idealistic. I wasn't ready for all the compromises of marriage, and to be fair to Bob, I was a little selfish and immature. But he was no better. He had no intention of compromising his way of life, either. He truly thought I ought to be content enough being his wife to close my eyes to his infidelities. Which, of course, I couldn't do."

"So the marriage ended."

"With relief on Bob's part and disillusionment on mine." She pursed her lips. "I guess that's the way Mark felt about marriage too. He seems genuinely fond of my mother to this day, but it just wasn't in him to be faithful to her, or to the other women who came after her. Maybe other women can put up with cheating for the sake of staying married, but I can't live that way. And that being so,"—she shrugged—"I doubt I'll ever marry again. What about you? Did you ever come close to marriage?"

"Once." Josh refilled their wine glasses and took a sip. "A girl in Houston. I thought Dana was everything I'd ever want in a wife— beautiful, intelligent and fun. She'd visited the ranch a couple of times when the house was under construction, and I thought she understood that this would be our home." He grimaced, remembering. "It turned out she just considered it a weekend sort of place. What she wanted was for me to go to work for her father in his investment firm so that we could be in Houston and live the glamorous sort of life she was used to. When I refused, she accused me of being unreasonable, of wanting to bury her in the country away from her family and friends, besides expecting her to live in semipoverty. I guess she was right," he added ruefully, "because I never could bring myself to take a country club membership more seriously than an honest day's work."

"I'm sorry," Kitty murmured.

"Don't be," Josh said grimly. "On the night she broke our engagement, she threw the ring in my face at a party, in front of about fifty people, then left with another man and spent the night with him."

Kitty gasped. Even Bob had never been that cruel, that blatantly obvious with his infidelities. She was so shocked she couldn't even think of any words to say in comfort. Her eyes spoke for her.

Josh saw the compassion in them and said lightly, "Oh, I was pretty bitter for a while, but now I see that it was for the best. I've come to realize this sort of life isn't for most women. Mark's last wife couldn't handle it either, even with that fine showplace of a home he has. She couldn't stand the isolation. Even my mother was never happy. I think the only woman I've ever known who was genuinely happy with this life is Ellie. And maybe Adam's wife," he amended thoughtfully.

"Is it possible," Kitty suggested gently, "that it was her relationship with your father that made your mother unhappy, rather than ranch life itself?"

Josh nodded. "That was a lot of it, all right. My father drank too much and they used to quarrel all the time. But that's enough about me," he said with a smile. "You're an enigma to me, Kitty."

"In what way?"

They had finished their meal and were carrying their plates back into the kitchen. "You don't seem like the sort of woman for the rugged life yourself, and I thought you wouldn't lift a finger to do anything while you're here. I figured the boredom would drive you away within a couple of days. Yet you've been working as hard as if it were your own livelihood. I have to admit I had you figured wrong."

Kitty began the washing up, but Josh stopped her. "I'll get that later," he said. "Let's have some coffee."

While he poured it, Kitty admitted, "I didn't expect to, but I like the ranch. Working outdoors has given me a sense of satisfaction I've never felt before. Maybe I was meant to be a country girl all along."

"Does that mean you'll be staying after all?" Josh asked as he carried their coffee into the living room.

They both sat down on the sofa and Kitty shook her head. "I can't. I have to get back to my job."

"It's just as well," Josh said. "The novelty would soon wear off and you'd start pining for the city lights."

"Perhaps." Kitty shrugged. "Anyway, there's no point in Mark and my pretending our relationship will ever be more than superficial. I'd feel like an intruder in his life if I stayed, and truthfully, I don't think Mark would be any more comfortable with the situation than I would. He'd soon feel I was cramping his style."

"You're determined to keep painting as black a

picture of him as you possibly can, aren't you?" Josh demanded. "Why can't you forgive him, forgive the past?"

Kitty's eyes darkened. "I may forgive, but I don't know how I can forget." She gazed into her cup, but saw instead the little girl she'd once been. "When I was seven, I was injured in a car accident and in the hospital several weeks. Mark said he'd come to see me as soon as he could get away." Her voice shook as old emotions welled up inside her, and the pain in her eyes was stark as she asked rhetorically, "Do you have any idea how intensely a seven-year-old can hope? Every day I prayed he'd walk through the door, but it never happened. He called once in a while and deluged my room with flowers and presents, but he never came."

"Kitty!" Josh's voice was filled with unmistakable compassion.

She held up a hand. "Don't!" She couldn't bear sympathy, even this many years later. She drew a deep breath and, with her emotions under control once more, recited the rest of the story in a matter-of-fact voice. "The same thing happened when I was twelve and had the lead in a school play, and again the night of my high school graduation. When he didn't bother to show up for that, I finally saw Mark as he really was—a selfish man who just didn't give a damn about me. Oh, he'd always sent the child-support payments and lavish gifts—easy enough things to do when you've got plenty of money. But he refused to give me the only gift I'd ever wanted . . . himself. He was too busy with his career, his trips around the world, his series of girlfriends and wives!"

Josh reached for her hand, but Kitty snatched it away. The frustrations and bitterness of the past overwhelmed her and she was desperately fighting tears. Angrily, she mopped at her eyes. "You've accused me of being a lousy daughter, and you're absolutely right! From the night of my graduation, I was finished with Mark Winters. After that I refused to talk to him on the phone or accept his letters or gifts, and when I got married I didn't bother to invite him to my wedding. Can you imagine how ridiculous I would have looked," she challenged, "if I'd counted on him to accompany me down the aisle? I'd have been left with egg on my face! Yet you wonder why I didn't want to come see him!"

"Kitty, Kitty, I hate seeing you so bitter," Josh said gently. "I didn't have such a great father either, but I didn't let it destroy my love for him."

"Well, mine wasn't around to love!" Kitty said with stinging vehemence. "He was only a face on a movie screen to me. What was I supposed to do? Adore him from afar like a groupie?"

"Give him a break," Josh pleaded. "Sure, Mark did wrong; I won't deny that. But you have to let go of the past and start again from the here and now. Mark isn't the same man he was back then, believe me! He's a decent, responsible, caring person—in fact, the kindest human being I've ever known. And he loves you, Kitty. He loves you." Suddenly he stood. "I've got something to show you," he said, crossing the room to the bookcase. He opened a door, took out something and returned to sit beside her.

In his hand he held a small blue velvet jeweler's box, and when he snapped it open, Kitty saw that it contained an exquisite pair of diamond earrings. "Mark had a Dallas jeweler visit him this week and he bought these for you," Josh told her. "He plans to give them to you the day he gets home from the hospital. I just thought it might be good for you to see them now."

"What does that prove?" Kitty snapped. "He's only doing what he's always done—trying to buy my affection with baubles. But I'm not an easily impressed child any longer." She looked away and chewed at her lower lip. "Tell him to return them and get his money back."

Josh snapped the lid shut on the box and dropped it into his pocket. "Obviously there's no way Mark can ever make things up to you because you don't want it!" His own voice was as hard and cold as the diamonds he'd just shown her. "You feel safer wrapped up in your resentment!"

"You're crazy!"

"Am I?" Josh went on ruthlessly. "You feel protected by your hatred. If you don't love somebody, then they can't hurt you, isn't that right? You even let the old hurts from your childhood spill over into the rest of your life. You had a dud of a husband, and because he cheated on you the way Mark did on your mother, you've branded all men as the same. Now no other man is allowed to get near you." His mouth twisted. "Everybody gets hurt somewhere along the line, but we don't all block out every overture of warmth and affection that's offered to us, just to keep from getting hurt again. Yet that's exactly what you're doing."

"So now you're a pop psychologist, are you?" Kitty shook with rage. "You're not qualified for the job, Joshua Steele, and I resent your trying to analyze me. You don't have the slightest idea what you're talking about!"

"Don't I?" Without warning, Josh snatched her into his arms. His eyes were narrowed and his mouth was grim. "I've wanted you since the first moment we met. And you've wanted me, too." Kitty squirmed, trying to free herself, but his arms only tightened around her and his face came nearer to hers—dangerously nearer. "You were honest about it once, but now whenever I come near you, you deliberately start a quarrel. I think it's nothing more than a defense. I'll admit I've had my hang-ups too. I've tried to deny to myself just how much I want you. But I'm saying it now. God only knows why, Kitty, because you're one of the most obstinate, disagreeable people I've ever met, but I've fallen for you, hard. The only thing I ever think about anymore is how very much I want to make love to you."

"No!" Kitty's voice caught on a breath of panic. She pressed her hand against the unyielding wall of his chest and turned her head so that she didn't have to look at him. "Don't," she pleaded. "Please, don't say these things."

The warmth of his body so near to hers was

seeping into her skin, into her consciousness, undermining her long-held resolve.

"Look at me," Josh ordered. His voice was filled with a rough anger. "Look at me and tell me you don't want me too."

"I don't!" she insisted. "I don't!" Kitty closed her eyes, fighting the weakness that was spreading through her. The heat of him, the enticing male scent of him were dreadful in their power. She dared not look at him because if she did, she knew she'd be lost.

Josh's lips went to her throat while at the same time his hands slipped beneath her sweater. The feel of his touch on her flesh was shattering, and as one hand crept upward over her rib cage and found a breast, Kitty groaned.

"Ah, Josh," she murmured. "Please don't do this. Don't make me want you."

His lips traveled up her chin to the corner of her mouth. His fingers were stroking the swell of her breast, sending her to the edge of capitulation. Kitty strained to hang on to her senses, to the hem of reason.

"I told you," he whispered against her lips, "you already do. Is it so terrible?"

"Yes, yes, terrible," she gasped, still stoically waging a battle against the sensations that were already beginning to topple logic from its pedestal.

"Why?"

"Because," she said. "Because . . . I can't remember." She was over the edge.

Josh chuckled with gentle amusement. "And

now," he said with satisfaction ringing in his voice, "tell me what I'm waiting to hear."

Kitty's body tingled with heightened desires; an urgent hunger throbbed and beat through her veins, an appetite that demanded to be assuaged. The battle was lost; the war had ended.

She sighed, opened her eyes at last and met the liquid softness in his gaze. "I want you to make love to me, Josh," she answered in defeat.

Chapter Eight

Twilight cast deepening shadows across the bedroom and the figures of the two lovers seemed as one, silhouetted as they were against the pale wall by the illumination of a single lamp.

Josh inhaled deeply, intoxicated by the sweet perfume of Kitty's hair. He embedded his fingers in the thick dark tresses, then bent his head to claim her soft lips.

He felt her go completely still for one brief instant, and then her lips parted in surrender. She touched his shoulders fleetingly, then his neck, and finally wound her fingers through his hair as the urgent sensations that stormed over him swept over her as well.

Josh crushed her to him until nothing separated them except their clothes. His tongue

played at the inner corners of her mouth, and
the delicious intimacy sent erotic currents puls-
ing through his veins. His body tensed and
hardened with desire.

Their intermingled breathing grew raspy and
uneven. Josh slid his hands down her back and
over the sensuous curve of her hips as Kitty's
fingers entwined around his neck. The kiss
ended, but their lips were almost touching as
they smiled.

"I think I've been looking for you all my life,"
he whispered. Once more his hands stroked her
magnificent hair, but Josh's eyes never left her
face. "I don't want to fight with you anymore."

"Neither do I," she answered shakily.

Wordlessly he took her hand and led her toward the bed. They lay across it and embraced
again. Josh kissed her over and over as though
her lips were a banquet. Kitty accepted his
kisses hungrily, responding with no thought beyond the wonder of the moment. For so very long
she had held herself under stern control, aloof
from the physical demands of her body. Now the
pent-up pressures exploded inside her. She
could no more have stopped the flood of sensations that charged her than she could have
halted a hurricane. What was now begun had to
be played out to the end.

Soon not even their clothes separated them,
and Josh's long, firm body warmed her bare
skin. When he drew back to look at her fully, the
admiration in his gaze heated her even more.

"I've been dreaming of you, you know," he
whispered hoarsely. "About how beautiful you

would be like this. But the reality far exceeds my poor imagination." His hands slid in gentle exploration from her slender white throat to the proud peaks of her firm breasts, then down to her hips. His breath caught at the utter perfection of her. She was womanhood in exquisite glory.

"I . . . I've dreamed of you, too," Kitty confessed softly.

"And?"

There was a hint of amused laughter in the word, but also a suspicion of anxiety lest she find him wanting. To Kitty, that was most endearing. She smiled, running her fingers across his chest and up to the strong, angular shoulders. "If you," she said, huskily, "didn't have quite such strong shoulders, *quite* such compelling eyes, *quite* such a firm and attractive physique, then maybe I would have succeeded in putting you out of my mind. Heaven knows I told myself often enough that you weren't worth a thought!"

Josh chuckled. He was adoring this girl more every moment. "You sound," he teased, "*quite* disgruntled."

"I am. I didn't want this, Josh," she said seriously.

"I know, sweetheart." He gave her a gentle, consoling kiss at the corner of her mouth. "I didn't either."

"Then why . . .?"

"Because we can't help ourselves," he whispered. "Because it was inevitable from the first moment we saw each other."

Kitty sighed, knowing he was right. It had been inevitable from the beginning.

Josh kissed her again, and this time it was neither gentle nor consoling. It was hot and demanding and forceful. It made her blood race, and Kitty forgot her questions and doubts in the rapturous present.

Josh's lovemaking was unhurried and thorough. He was an artist, she the canvas; the paints were the varied sensations that spread over her, tingling and delicious, making her go hot and cold and all the shades of temperature in between; his hands were the brushstrokes, sure and confident as they touched her with the expertise of genius.

Never in all her life had Kitty been so acutely aware of the magnificent wonder that was her own body. It was so sensitive to the lightest touch of his fingertips, finely tuned to the most fleeting pressure of his firm lips. She was sharply aware of the feathery gentleness of his breath against her skin. She thrilled, she ached, she yearned, she throbbed, but still the sweet torment continued.

Josh sensed instinctively that for Kitty, this was an entirely new experience. The little smile of pleasure on her lips, the tiny gasps of excited delight and surprise gave her away, though he wasn't consciously aware of it. He only knew that despite the torture of his own needs, he must be patient. Her happiness, her satisfaction, had suddenly become the most important things in the world to him.

But then Kitty surprised him. Though in the
beginning she had seemed so uncertain of her
own caresses, so amazed at his, all at once she
became aggressive and bold. She dotted kisses
on his chest, stroked his thigh, nibbled on his
fingertips and altogether began, slowly and very
deliberately, to drive him mad.

Always Josh had yearned for such a woman—a
wild, untamed creature who would give as well
as take, demand as well as submit, possess as
well as be possessed, a woman who staked her
claim. And at last, unbelievably, he had found
her. She played havoc with his self-restraint as
she swept his face and chest with her hair. She
kissed the pulse at his throat and let her fingers
dance along his rib cage. She teased him and
laughed as she imprisoned his hands so that he
could not touch her while she had her way. He
was utterly tantalized by her frenzied movements, incredulous with delight at her natural,
uninhibited sensuality.

But when his passion became excruciating, he
halted her little game and became once more
the tigress's master.

He pulled her to him, and Kitty's heart thud-
ded at the light in his eyes. They glinted so
fiercely, glowing with fire, that she quivered
with breathless anticipation. Her own wild
needs matched the primitive ruthlessness of his,
and as he pushed her to the pillows and came
down to her at last, she was more than ready.

They fitted together with overwhelming urgency. Kitty thought she must die from the pain

of unreleased passion that clouded her mind. She was now but an object of feelings, of torturous sensations.

Then she ceased to think at all. The delectable, sweet agony was too great. Every atom of her body was focused only on the shattering ecstasy that came at last. She cried out again and again and shuddered against Josh's damp chest as the vortex swirled seemingly without end.

Slowly the aftershocks grew fewer, milder, less devastating, and the lovers lay quiet and limp. Josh continued to hold her long afterward, reluctant even in exhaustion to let her go. It had been too extraordinary, too precious an occasion, and the stunning realization continued to rock through him. More than mere lovemaking, they had seemed to become linked within their minds and hearts and even their very souls.

He lifted a hand and brushed it across her moist brow. "You are," he said finally, "very, very special, Kitty." It wasn't at all what he'd wanted to say, but the words that were inscribed on his heart stayed there, hidden in the darkness. Affected as he was by this woman, by what had just happened between them, he could not bring himself yet to express aloud what he was truly feeling.

Kitty fought tears that burned her throat. She wasn't sure precisely what she had hoped he'd say, but "special" seemed woefully inadequate for what had just happened to her. He had been the sun and the moon and all the stars for her, and he had called her merely special. Now she felt like a total fool. The sooner she got away from there, the better!

Helplessly, Josh saw her withdraw inside herself even as she physically withdrew from his arms.

"Thanks," she said flippantly. She turned her back to him and swung her legs off the bed.

Josh moved quickly. He gently placed his hands on her shoulders, stopping her from getting up. "I've hurt you somehow," he said softly. "And I didn't mean to. Kitty, I'm not so good with words, but what just happened was more than wonderful for me. It was far beyond my dreams and that's important. I hope it meant as much to you."

Kitty bowed her head and her voice was thick. "I can't . . . I . . . can't talk about it."

"Why not?"

Kitty shook her head. "Because I don't know how."

Josh's hands gripped her shoulders more tightly. There was a small silence, and then he asked, "Are words so hard for you, too?"

Mutely, she nodded.

Gently Josh turned her to face him. "Then I think we have to find the words we need," he said firmly. "Was it good for you?"

Kitty closed her eyes to block out the piercing intensity of his, and huskily she admitted, "Too . . . too good."

"How can it be too good?" For the first time, he sounded amused.

Kitty opened her eyes and glared at him. "Because nothing can come of it, that's why. I'll be leaving soon and that will be the end of it. We'll never see each other again."

Josh shook his head. "That's one of the things we have to discuss. Stay, Kitty. Mark wants you to, and so do I." When she started to object he said sharply, "Hear me out, will you? What . . ." He halted, searching for the right words. "What just happened was unusual, don't you realize that? For it to be that fantastic between two people . . . well, it's just priceless! You can't leave now! I've got just as many reservations about us as you do, but something important is happening and we can't go back and pretend we don't have these feelings. Spend a few months here, get to know your father . . . and me. Let's find out what the natural conclusion of all this is."

Kitty stunned him by her angry reaction. "What you've just said is all the more reason for me to go. Before either of us gets hurt!"

"What are you talking about? You're not being fair!"

"I've found," Kitty retorted, "that life generally isn't fair!" She pulled away from him and moved across the room, gathering her discarded clothes.

"Why are you doing this?" Josh said hotly. "Don't you think we'll both be hurt if you go away now?"

"Maybe," Kitty said in a choked voice. "But not as much as if I stayed. And the pain *would* come, Josh, sooner or later. Men don't stay faithful to any one woman. It just isn't in them. You're interested in me now, but I don't intend to stick around until your interest wanes. I just . . . I just can't handle that scene again."

Josh's voice was filled with barely controlled fury. "You must be very insecure to feel you can't hold a man's interest. But then, you're probably right," he added cruelly. "Any woman who's as cold-blooded and selfish as you could never hold *me* for long. So maybe the sooner you're gone from here, the better off we'll both be!"

The following morning Kitty was still so despondent that it was all she could do to whip up the proper amount of enthusiasm when Mark telephoned to say he'd be discharged on Friday. She was truly glad for him, but his coming home made her leaving that much closer. She'd promised to stay on a day or two beyond that, and that meant she'd be on a Chicago-bound plane by Monday—Tuesday at the latest.

She ought to be eager to leave. After all, she'd never wanted to come in the first place, and she'd been adamant about not remaining for months on end. But now that the time was almost upon her, she hated the thought of it.

For going meant never seeing Josh again.

Not that he'd ever want to see her again anyway, after last night. He'd even said so. And it was entirely her fault, her decision, she thought miserably, that had brought about the situation. Logically, she knew she'd been right. Getting involved with Josh would only lead to the disaster of pain.

But, an inner voice insisted, she was already involved and she already felt pain. So what had she accomplished except to bring that pain about just that much sooner?

Last night Josh had taught her the true meaning of being a woman. Funny how she'd believed herself to be a thoroughly modern, up-to-date woman, and yet until then she hadn't realized how little she actually knew about lovemaking. She'd had no idea how truly glorious it could be. For all Bob's reputation as a lady-killer, he had never made her feel the way Josh had. Josh had been exciting, making her feel beautiful and desirable, and he'd been as interested in her pleasure as in his own. He had brought her an indescribable satisfaction, a wondrous feeling of completion she'd never before known—a feeling she now feared she might never again experience.

But such thoughts only made her feel worse. Kitty decided she needed some fresh air to blow them away. She slipped on a jacket, got the broom from the utility room and carried it through the house. Yesterday she'd noticed that the strong wind had littered the front porch with leaves and twigs.

She'd scarcely begun when an unfamiliar blue car pulled into the drive. A young woman about her own age, dressed neatly in a vivid green sweater and skirt, emerged from the car. She had short strawberry blonde hair, bright hazel eyes that glowed with good humor, and an engaging smile.

"Hi. I'm Carol Robbins."

"Ellie's daughter-in-law." Kitty smiled back. "I'm Kitty Peterson. It's nice to meet you. Come in and I'll make some coffee."

"Actually, what I had in mind was lunch," Carol said. "Ellie's babysitting for me today and I'm going into Brownwood to do some shopping. I thought you might like to come along. It'll give us a chance to get acquainted. I'll even," she added persuasively, "spring for lunch."

Kitty laughed, deciding she was going to like Carol. "Now that's an offer I can't refuse. Just let me change my clothes."

Twenty minutes later they were wending their way along the twisting rural road out to the highway. In the distance Kitty could see a mountain range with flat-topped mesas. Carol told her they were the Comanche Mountains.

A few minutes later, as they passed through the tiny community of May, Carol pointed out the road leading to her parents' house. "They're retired peanut farmers. Now they enjoy traveling and, whenever they're home, spoiling my son." Grinning, she added, "Little Adam's the only grandchild on both sides of the family, so in another year he'll probably be so rotten we won't be able to live with him."

Kitty laughed. "I guess that's the price you have to pay for all those free babysitters."

Carol nodded, then said, "Tell me about your job at the boutique. It would never do for me to work in a place like that. I'd be tempted to spend all my paycheck right there."

Kitty described her work, confided her ambition to own a similar shop herself someday, and amused Carol with stories of some of her ample-figured, matronly customers and the strangely juvenile fashion choices they made. Carol was a good audience, as was Kitty, who listened in delight to humorous accounts of the disasters created by the energetic little Adam. The two women talked nonstop on the drive, and by the time they entered Brownwood, they had become fast friends.

"I promised Ellie I'd stop by her lawyer's office to pick up a real estate contract for her," Carol said. "We'll go there first and then we'll be free as the birds."

She turned off the Early Highway and abruptly they plunged into the narrow, congested streets of the original downtown area of the city. Weathered stone buildings lined the streets that converged on the courthouse square. The courthouse itself was a large, red brick structure set amid tall shade trees.

Carol found a place to park and, while Kitty waited in the car, ran her errand. She was soon back and they were on their way, winding through the downtown business district and past a modern post office.

"While we're over this way, I'll take you past Howard Payne University."

"I'd like that," Kitty said.

The university was a cluster of red brick build-

ings surrounded by neat, green lawns and pleasant trees. A number of students were walking to
classes while others sat on the lawn, enjoying
the fine day.

"Josh told me he attended classes here," Kitty
said. Instantly she regretted having brought up
his name. Ever since Carol had arrived at the
house, she had put the thought of him aside.
Now the pain came back afresh.

"So did Adam and I," Carol said. "Speaking of
Josh," she went on, "did Ellie tell you I want to
have you both to dinner one night while you're
here?"

"She told me," Kitty said dully, "but it
wouldn't be a very good idea."

"Why not?" Carol looked at her, and the anguish in Kitty's eyes gave her swift understanding. "Oh. I see. I'm sorry."

Kitty managed a wan smile. "So am I."

"Josh is a terrific person," Carol ventured.

Kitty swallowed. "I know," she said quietly.

"I suppose you also know he and Adam are
close friends. All the same, I'm quite good
at keeping confidences. If you ever need an
ear . . ." Carol left the offer dangling.

"Thanks. I'll remember that," Kitty said. She
knew instinctively that she could trust Carol,
but for now her relationship with Josh, her
ambivalent feelings for him, and the hurt she
felt were all too new for her to be able to put
them into words. To take both their minds off it,
she said abruptly, "Mark's coming home Friday
and I'd like to throw him a welcome-home party.
Think we could pick up some decorations and

food? Also champagne. I promised him champagne."

Carol smiled. "We'll get the works. We'll stop at the bakery first and order a cake. My treat."

The party was a success. Colorful balloons festooned the ceiling, a Welcome Home banner decorated a wall and there was plenty of food. Mark was ebullient to be home and demonstrated for everyone how well he could hobble around on crutches.

It was a festive occasion, even though Kitty had kept the guest list small so that Mark wouldn't grow overexcited or tired. A few of his closest friends from Rising Star and Cross Plains were there as well as his friend Ken from Abilene. Oakie and Red were also there, of course, along with Ellie, Carol and Adam Robbins.

And Josh.

Kitty had known she couldn't possibly leave him out, but she hadn't had the nerve to call and invite him. Though it made her feel cowardly, she'd asked Carol do it for her.

All evening Kitty had done her best to stay out of his vicinity without making it obvious. Not that it had been very difficult. Josh seemed equally intent on avoiding her.

"Kitty," Mark said, suddenly commanding her attention. "See that everyone has a glass of champagne, would you? I have an important announcement to make."

Kitty moved around the room, refilling glasses. When she came to Josh, her hand shook a little as she poured the bubbly liquid into his glass. When she finished, she quickly passed on to the next person without ever meeting his eyes.

Mark was seated in an easy chair with his leg propped on an ottoman. As everyone fell expectantly silent, he held out his hand to Ellie. She moved to his side, and as they clasped hands, they shared a secret smile.

Mark cleared his throat and in his best stage voice thundered, "Ladies and gentlemen, I'd like to introduce you to my future wife."

There was an immediate clamor of laughter, applause and congratulations. Mark's intense gaze was on his daughter's face. "All right?" it seemed to ask.

Kitty smiled and blew a kiss to Ellie. "All right," she answered in the same silent language. Her approval was wholehearted because she sincerely liked Ellie. If any woman would be right for Mark, she was the one. Natural and unaffected, Ellie would help a man keep his feet firmly planted on the ground. As for Mark, she realized that a lot of what Josh had told her was true. He wasn't the flighty film star he'd once been. There was a depth and stability to him now. She sincerely hoped they would have a good marriage.

Suddenly Kitty felt a strong, magnetic pull and knew Josh was looking at her. She resisted him while she congratulated the newly engaged couple, admired the stunning engagement ring Ellie displayed and drank a toast along with the rest of the guests.

Adam Robbins came to her and kissed Kitty's

cheek. "Welcome to the family. Do you approve of the merger?"

"Indeed I do. And you?" She thought of Mark's dismal track record.

He nodded. "Mom and Mark have been good friends for years. They ought to know their own minds by now. I honestly think they'll be happy together."

"I hope so."

Adam grinned. "Well, little sis, if you ever need me to beat up any bullies for you, let me know."

"Thanks, big brother," Kitty laughed. "I'll remember that. I must say it'll be very nice being an aunt to little Adam. He's a charmer. Yesterday when Carol was here, he—" She was interrupted when Mark called for silence again.

"Come on, Mark," Adam joked, "enough of these dramatic scenes. You're not on Broadway here, you know!"

Mark chuckled good-naturedly. "I know. I'll try to be brief and not get too maudlin. Kitty, come here."

She knew immediately that Mark was about to present her with the earrings Josh had shown her. She hadn't anticipated its being done so publicly, and as she moved to his side, she fretted over how to refuse gracefully.

"These are for you, Kitten," Mark began. "Not everyone here is aware of what a damn fool I was for most of your life, afraid to be a father, mostly afraid of failing at being a father. So I just . . . avoided the job altogether. Not only did I do myself out of the best thing the world has to

offer—watching my daughter grow up and earning your love and respect—but I ended up hurting you. I had no right to expect you even to give
me the time of day, yet you came to me when I
was ill. I know it wasn't easy for you to do, but
I'm grateful that you did. I just hope someday
you can forgive me for the past. So . . . this is for
you, a small token of my love. And I do love you,
Kitten. Very much."

Kitty hadn't expected the speech and the im-
pact of it hit her hard. She gazed numbly at the
lovely, winking diamonds and swallowed with
difficulty. When she finally looked at Mark, the
earnest tenderness in his gaze upset her emotional balance even more. Abruptly, without
knowing she would, she quietly laid down her
battle shield.

Struggling to hide the depths of her feelings,
she blinked rapidly to hold back the tears that
burned her eyes. Half laughing, half crying, she
snapped roughly, "Oh, damn it, I love you too,
Daddy. I always have."

The others laughed at her brusque manner,
but Mark wasn't fooled or put off. He opened his
arms, and for the first time in twenty-four years,
father and daughter embraced.

Ellie hugged her next and whispered, "I knew
it would happen. I had faith in you both. You just
made one man very, very happy, Kitty."

Kitty laughed huskily. "I imagine you've
made him even happier. I'm glad you're going to
be his wife, Ellie. When's the wedding?"

"On Valentine's Day," Ellie replied. "Kitty,
Mark and I would both like you to stay on and

live with us. But failing that, will you at least consider staying until the wedding? It would mean so much to both of us."

Kitty became thoughtful. Beside her, her father touched her hand and said one word: "Please."

She wavered. The wedding was a month away. If she stayed, it would definitely mean losing her job and starting over somewhere else. It also meant she'd be forced into situations where she'd have to see Josh, an intolerable prospect. Tonight had proved how awkward and difficult that could be.

She sighed and promised reluctantly, "I'll think about it."

"Fair enough." Mark's heartiness was forced and Kitty knew he was disappointed.

Overwhelmed by the emotions of last half hour, Kitty felt a need to be alone. When she thought herself unobserved, she slipped through the kitchen and out the back door. She grabbed a sweater on her way and wrapped it around her shoulders as she walked across the lawn to a chair swing.

The night air crept around her, pressing cold, clammy fingers on her arms and legs and throat. She welcomed the blast of frosty air that cooled her face, for it had been hot and flushed all evening from the self-conscious strain of being in the same room with Josh.

A sudden movement in the darkness startled her. From the deep shadows of the black trees, a tall, familiar form stepped forward.

Josh dropped down beside her and the swing

surged forward, then back. "Well, well," he said, breaking the tense silence, "what a charming little hypocrite you are! When I showed you the earrings, you were so indignant at Mark's attempt to buy your affections. Yet tonight, how sweetly you accepted them and told Daddy how much you loved him. It's nothing but a big lie!"

"It wasn't a lie!" Kitty exclaimed defensively. "I do love him. It's just been hard to deal with my feelings for him after all these years, that's all."

"Are you going to stay for the wedding?"

She shook her head. "Probably not. I'd like to, but I'll lose my job if I do."

"And we know," Josh sneered, "that's more important than Mark."

"What's it to you?" Kitty demanded angrily. "I thought you were anxious for me to leave."

Josh shrugged. "It doesn't matter to me one way or the other. The only thing that matters is your deception of Mark with that loving-daughter act. He doesn't deserve that. As for us, if you do stay, I'm sure we can manage to be civil in front of the others and avoid each other the rest of the time."

As abruptly as he'd come, he stood up and walked away.

Kitty sensed the hurt beneath his sarcasm. Impulsively she called out. "Josh?"

His body was almost indistinct in the darkness, but she saw him stop, though he didn't turn. She licked her lips and said, "I'm . . . I'm really sorry about everything. Between us, I mean. I hurt you and I didn't mean to. But I still think it's for the best."

Josh came back a few steps. Kitty could just see the outline of his face in the half-light. "I've already realized that," he said curtly, "so don't let it trouble you. All I am is a struggling rancher trying to make ends meet. I don't have the financial means to satisfy a woman like you."

Kitty was appalled and she leaped to her feet. "How can you say that?" she cried. "This has nothing to do with money."

He smiled grimly. "Doesn't it?" he asked with brutal coldness. "I can't possibly give you beautiful things like those diamonds Mark gave you tonight. The same diamonds you scorned at first. But I guess you've had time to think things over and realize how foolish you'd be to refuse such a valuable gift—even if you have no use for the sentiments behind them."

Kitty stepped forward and slapped him hard. Her throat throbbed with pain and fury. "You're jealous!" she accused. "You've been close to Mark for so long that you've come to regard yourself as heir apparent! You resent the fact that Mark and I have made up, because now you're relegated to the role of a mere employee again!"

"That's a lie!" Josh grated harshly. Enraged, he grabbed her, crushing her to him as he brutally kissed her.

There was nothing in the least loverlike about his kiss. It was punishing and rough as he expended but a fraction of his anger upon her.

Kitty trembled and could scarcely breath, and though she struggled, she could not free herself.

Then, just as abruptly as the assault had begun, it ended. Josh thrust her from him, and his eyes were hard, cold flints as his gaze raked her face with frank contempt. Kitty shivered, chilled by it.

"Go back to the party and play the prodigal," he told her. "You know, you ought to be in movies yourself. You're every bit as good at acting as your father. You certainly convinced him with your adoring-daughter act. And the other night—for a little while—you had me convinced you really cared about me. But I see through the act now. You're just an ice woman without a heart!"

Chapter Nine

Over a fresh pot of coffee the next morning, the upcoming wedding was under discussion. Ellie had joined Mark and Kitty for breakfast and Kitty was openly amused at the engaged pair's wrangling over where the event was to take place. Ellie opted for a simple ceremony in her house with only the immediate family and a half dozen close friends present. Mark, on the other hand, wanted it to be in the nearby community church, as elegant as possible, inviting a multitude of friends and topping it with a formal dinner-dance reception at a private club in Brownwood. They demanded that Kitty be judge and jury, a task she wisely refused.

"Oh, no, you don't! You'll have to fight this one out yourselves. If I took sides, whoever lost would be my enemy for life."

"Coward," Ellie said.

Her father made a clucking sound like a chicken. The accusation was obvious.

"Sticks and stones, et cetera," Kitty said with a laugh, holding up her hands. "Sorry, folks, but no matter what you call me, I'm not getting embroiled in this argument."

"Have you thought over whether or not you'll stay for it?" Mark asked.

Kitty sighed. "Dad, I'd like to, honestly. But if I do, I'll lose my job, and I just can't afford that."

"You know money's no problem," he said quietly. "I'll give you an allowance as long as you need it until you find another one. That checking account is still in your name, you know. Besides, Ellie and I were serious about wanting you to stay for good, if you found you liked it here. You could have a job with me."

Kitty stared at him. "Doing what?"

"You could work with Josh and learn to handle my business affairs. It would mean some traveling, but you're young; you could handle that. It's gotten to the point that Josh is overloaded and has to be away from his ranch more than he likes. I'm sure he'd welcome some relief and a bit more free time. And I'd like you to learn the ins and outs of it all, anyway. Someday most of it will be yours."

"It's out of the question for me to accept your offer," Kitty said quietly. "I have a life of my own already in Chicago."

"Of course," Mark said. "I'm being selfish. Naturally you want to live close to Jeanne."

"It's not just Mom," Kitty explained. "All my

friends are there; all my interests are there. Chicago is home to me."

Mark knew nothing, of course, about the situation between her and Josh, so she couldn't tell him the real reason for her refusal . . . that working with Josh would be impossible. The truth was, his offer was tempting and the job sounded a lot more interesting than the one she had. She concealed her own disappointment in the face of his, and because she honestly hated hurting him, she said quickly, before she could change her mind, "We'll compromise. I'll accept your offer of an allowance until I can find another job, and I'll stay for the wedding. But as soon as it's over, I'll be going back."

Mark smiled, and though Kitty dreaded the idea of remaining so near to Josh for another month, she knew she'd made the right decision. The look on her father's face told her how much she had pleased him, even before he exclaimed, "That's my girl!" He turned swiftly to Ellie and stated, "Now we have to have a church wedding. That way you can have Carol and Kitty both as your bridal attendants."

"I'm delighted Kitty's staying," Ellie said, "but she can just as easily be my attendant in a home ceremony."

Kitty stood up and grinned. "Same act, scene two. I'll leave you to hash this out. I'd better go telephone my boss and tell her to replace me."

In the privacy of her bedroom, her mask of cheerfulness dropped as she sank onto the window seat and looked out at the gloomy winter morning. Staying for the wedding unquestionably made Mark and Ellie happy, but it also meant that now she had no choice but to accept temporary financial support from Mark, much as she hated to do it. It also would give Josh more ammunition for his accusation that she was mercenary. To him, it would constitute proof that he'd been right about her. The anticipation of his scorn was painful.

But then, Kitty told herself impatiently, what difference did it make what Joshua Steele thought of her? It shouldn't matter at all.

A jackrabbit scurried from behind a bush and hopped around the corner of the house. The sight should have pleased her, but instead her eyes clouded and a cold, heavy despondency crashed down upon her as she realized that it did matter—greatly—what Josh thought of her. She was in love with him. The thing she'd dreaded most and wanted to avoid at all costs had happened.

How cruelly ironic life was, she thought, and what a fool she'd been! She'd tried so hard to hold her emotions in check, to keep herself from falling in love with him so she wouldn't be hurt again, and now the worst was upon her despite her precautions. How had she let it happen? And what was she going to do now?

Josh not only did not return her love, he actually despised her. Kitty shivered as a cold chill seeped through her. She'd done irreparable damage that night when she'd rejected his affections and turned them into hate, while all she'd meant to do was save them both from the anguish she was now suffering. Now it was too late to go back and start afresh. She had destroyed forever whatever tender feelings he'd once had for her.

Josh's mood had been black for days. He'd avoided association with other people and put in long, hard hours at the ranch where he could let off steam. But finally he couldn't bear his own company any longer, and so this morning he'd driven to Cross Plains.

Around noon, after he'd finished loading the supplies he'd purchased at the feed store, he decided he might as well have lunch before heading home.

The small restaurant faced the highway that ran through the center of town. Josh parked in front of it, and after exchanging a few pleasantries with Bert, an acquaintance who was just coming out, he headed in for lunch. He stopped near the counter to let his eyes adjust to the dim interior and idly glanced around. He knew just about everybody in town, and normally it was easy to find a lunch companion.

That's when he saw her, tucked away alone in the last booth in the back. Her lovely blue-black hair fanned about her face and she wore a becoming tomato red shirtdress.

Josh's heart lurched. How long, he asked himself, had he loved her? Since that cold evening when he'd seen her in a Chicago exercise studio? The time he'd seen her all wet and muddy after working all day in the pasture? Or was it only since the night they'd made love?

But it did no good to think about that night.

That was only self-inflicted torture. Kitty had made it plain enough that she wanted no part of him. He wavered now between wanting to go to her and feeling impelled to leave quickly before she was aware of his presence. Just when he was about to follow the impulse to leave, Kitty saw him.

She appeared as surprised as he was. Her lips parted and for a long, timeless moment their gazes clung. The surroundings, the voices and clatter of dishes, ceased to exist; Josh was only aware of Kitty, of his aching need of her, and of the raw pain that was so plainly evident in her eyes.

Like a magnet inexorably drawing him, he went to her. By the time he reached her, he saw that her defenses had gone up. The anguish that had been in her gaze only a moment ago was gone; now the brown eyes were murky, unfathomable pools concealing the emotions behind them, and he remembered the deliberately cruel things he'd said to her the night of Mark's party.

As though that night hadn't happened and the ugly words never said, Josh nodded pleasantly. "Hello."

"Hello." Kitty's voice was anything but inviting.

"I talked with Mark on the phone this morning. He said you've decided to stay for the wedding."

"That's right." Kitty's body was rigid, her gaze cool.

"You've made him very happy."

Kitty shrugged. "Of course it meant giving up

my job and living off Mark's money for a while. I guess you expect me to congratulate you for being right."

"Right?"

"Certainly. About how mercenary I am. How I'm taking advantage of him."

Her hostility was razor sharp. Uninvited, Josh sat down opposite her and without hesitation leaned forward to clasp her hands. His voice was soft and urgent. "I don't blame you for hating me. I've been kicking myself ever since I said those things. My only defense is that I was hurt and angry. I didn't really mean it, Kitty. Can you forgive me?"

He looked so stricken that Kitty was forced to believe the apology was genuine. It eased some of the soreness around her heart. She hesitated, then flipped her hands palms up and laced her fingers between his. "If you can forgive me, too. I didn't mean what I said either, Josh. About your being jealous and resenting my place with Mark. As for slapping you, I . . . I . . ." Her voice broke and she bent her head in shame.

Josh removed one hand from hers and tipped her chin so that she had to look at him. The warmth of his smile radiated through her. "Apologies all around," he said cheerfully. "Now, can we change the subject so I can tell you how beautiful you are today?"

Kitty laughed softly. "You may."

Josh squeezed her hands, then released them, afraid to push his luck too far, too fast. "Consider yourself told. I like that shade of red on you."

"Thank you." Kitty liked the way he looked,

too, but this unexpected meeting and the even more unexpected friendliness between them was too tenuous a thing yet, and she felt strangely shy. She could hardly say that the sight of him sent tingles through her, that she loved the way his hair grew thick and rebelliously curly in one spot just over his forehead, that his smile made her heart do silly flips. That would be giving away her deepest feelings. She contented herself instead with quietly enjoying his presence. Her eyes feasted on his face, the shape of his shoulders beneath the blue shirt, the fine, lean strength of his arms and hands.

"Hi, Josh. It's good to see you," said a voice above them.

The attractive waitress who'd already taken Kitty's order had arrived with a menu for Josh. Although Kitty had rather liked her earlier, now she felt a sick dread in her stomach as she watched Josh smile at her.

"Hi, Janie," he said easily. "How'd Tommy make out at the rodeo last week in the calf roping?"

"He came in second. He sure was pleased with himself."

"Great! I knew he could do it. Tell him I'm proud of him."

"Why don't you tell him yourself? The Hanleys are having a little get-together tonight. Why don't you come with me, and when you stop by the house you can see Tommy's ribbon."

Josh shook his head. "Thanks, but I've already got plans tonight. With this lady." Josh smiled and nodded at Kitty.

The waitress shrugged and said good-naturedly, "Well, now, Josh, I didn't know you were taken."

He grinned and his gaze swept to Kitty's face. "I am," he declared solemnly. "Very taken." Then he introduced the two women.

Kitty was flustered over the circumstances, but Janie didn't seem to be at all upset that Josh had turned down her invitation. "You're new around here, aren't you?" Janie asked conversationally.

Kitty nodded. "I'm visiting my father."

"Mark Winters," Josh elaborated.

Janie's face suddenly beamed. "Mr. Winters is wonderful . . . not stuck up at all because he's famous. Once, when I was bringing my son Tommy home from a doctor's appointment in Brownwood, I had a flat tire on the highway. Your father came along and stopped and changed it for me." She giggled. "Now, how many people can say a superstar ever changed a tire for them? How is he since his accident?"

Kitty responded suitably, but her mind was a confused whirl. Here was yet another story about Mark Winters, the kindhearted and friendly neighbor. She was constantly having to revise her mental picture of him. Clearly, the man who'd callously ignored his young daughter no longer existed. She was glad that they were getting to know one another, that she'd buried the hatchet, because she did indeed love him. But it was still hard for her to see him as the man he'd become.

She was also confused about something else.

Janie had been all set to flirt with Josh when she'd first come to the table. That had been plain enough. But Josh had surprised Kitty. He had not, as her ex-husband would have done, flirted back. In fact, he'd said he was taking her out tonight. But then, she thought cynically, perhaps he simply didn't like Janie and had used the first fib he could think of to get out of the situation.

That thought sunk her into a gloomy state of mind. By the time Janie left and they were alone together again, Kitty could scarcely bring herself to look at Josh.

There was a small silence; she heard Josh shift his position slightly, but still Kitty refused to look up.

"Are you going to make a liar out of me?" Josh asked after a time.

In spite of her reluctance, Kitty raised her eyes. "About our nonexistent plans for tonight?"

A tiny grin quirked the corners of Josh's mouth. "It could be true if you'll have dinner with me."

The teasing gleam in his eyes was enticing, but Kitty was still wary. "Is she"—she inclined her head slightly in the direction of the counter —"one of your girlfriends?"

Josh's grin broadened. "I guess I could try to impress you by saying she's one of many, but the truth is there are none. Janie and I are just friends. Her husband was a school buddy of mine, and he died in an accident a couple of years ago. Once in a while I spend time with her nine-year-old son, Tommy, teaching him a few old football tricks or going to junior rodeos with him. I'm telling you the truth, Kitty. Now answer me, will you have dinner with me? I'm going away on business tomorrow and I'd really like to be with you tonight."

Kitty was dismayed at the news. "How . . . how long will you be gone?" Josh's eyes widened, and she knew he had heard the catch in her voice, that she'd given herself away.

"Probably a week. A week and a half at the most."

"I . . . I see," she murmured.

"I'll miss you, Kitty."

She took courage from his words. "I'll miss you, too," she admitted.

"And tonight?"

Kitty smiled and nodded. "I'd like to see you tonight."

Josh wished he knew what she was really thinking, whether she would miss him as much as he knew he'd miss her. Experimentally, lightly, he said, "You know, if we're not careful we could make a bad mistake."

"Such as?"

"Like falling in love with each other."

Josh watched closely for her reaction, and he was disappointed when he couldn't read her expression. Kitty's face gave away nothing as she replied with equal flippancy, "Surely we're too bright for that."

That evening they drove to Brownwood for dinner. Josh took a different route from the one Kitty had taken with Carol Robbins. This one carried them through hilly terrain and across Lake Brownwood, its shores dotted with motels, boat docks and a huge state park.

Over dinner, in response to Kitty's curious questions, Josh described some of Mark's business holdings. There were warehouses and apartment complexes in Los Angeles, where he was flying tomorrow, a motel in Sacramento, an office building in Boston, part ownership of a baseball team, two radio stations and one television station, all in far-flung parts of the country.

"I had no idea Mark was involved in so many different enterprises," Kitty said in stunned surprise.

"What did you think he had?"

She shook her head. "I don't know. Maybe an apartment building or a couple of rental houses . . . nothing on the scale you've described."

Josh touched her hand and said ruefully, "I'll have to revise my jaded opinion of your mercenary interest in Mark, won't I? Since you didn't even know what he owned."

Kitty laughed softly. "I hope it'll be in my favor."

His smile made her heart leap. "Oh, it's definitely in your favor," he answered. The expression in his eyes became so disturbing that she had to look away.

A few million stars and a jaunty half-moon littered the sky on their return journey. The evening had been perfect—delicious food, a relaxing atmosphere, mellowing wine. Mind had met mind, smile had brought forth smile, hand had touched hand. Neither wanted the time together to end, and in an unconscious effort to delay it, Josh drove slowly, taking deserted country roads.

His right arm circled Kitty's shoulder, and she was content to have it there as they talked idly of unimportant things. Both of them were trying to pretend that a long parting wasn't near, but neither quite succeeded. By degrees, they fell silent as dread and despair over their imminent separation robbed them of the pleasure they'd shared all evening. Now each was suddenly plunged into a secret, private unhappiness where the other could not go.

At a crossroads, Josh came to a stop. There were no sign posts in the dark wilderness, but he knew these roads like the back of his own hand. To the right, the road lead to his house; a left turn would take them to Mark Winters's home.

He glanced down at Kitty. Her face was a smooth alabaster silhouette against the black night. "Will you come home with me?" he asked simply.

Kitty's heart skipped and her throat went dry. She knew Josh wanted to make love to her. It was there in the fire of his eyes, evident in his quiet words, thrillingly apparent in the gentle touch of his hand as he stroked her cheek.

But she had to refuse. Her words were disjointed as she said regretfully, "I don't think that's a good idea. Josh, we . . . things have moved too fast between us already. We've gotten too serious and . . . it scares me."

"You're damned right I'm serious!" Josh exploded. Now both his hands cupped her face. His eyes were twin fiery coals, warming her skin with his emotions. "Darling, I know you're afraid of getting hurt again. I'm no masochist myself and I don't go around looking for pain either, but it's a chance we all take in this life simply because we're human. All I know is that I'm crazy about you, that I want you so badly it's almost like a sickness. If my feelings for you mean that somewhere down the line I have to get hurt, then I'm willing to take that risk!"

"Well, I'm not!" Kitty retorted. "Look at us. We fight all the time, or else we're falling into each other's arms. It's exhausting and confusing. Oh, Josh, I'm so mixed up! I want you, I honestly do, but I'm just not sure where all this is leading and I really believe we both need to do a bit of clear thinking. While you're away, it'll be a good opportunity for us to do that."

Josh's voice went strangely quiet and the flatness of it was more terrible than if he'd shouted at her in anger. "It seems to me that wanting each other . . . now . . . ought to be enough. What is it you're demanding of me, Kitty? A written guarantee for the future? An ironclad contract promising you eternal happiness and freedom from pain? A marriage proposal?"

Kitty was horrified. She recoiled violently, jerking away from his touch. "No! Never! The last thing I'm looking for is another husband!"

"What you mean," Josh said bitterly, "is that I'*m* not the husband you're looking for. Not that I blame you. I'm not a very good marriage risk."

"Why?" Kitty shot back with equal bitterness. "Because you know you wouldn't be faithful?"

"That would be dead easy with the right woman," Josh snapped impatiently. "I'm just not sure you're that woman. You're too hot-tempered, and you're certainly not the sort to be satisfied with the hand-to-mouth existence I'd have to offer."

Instant rage flowed through Kitty like a boiling river. "You've got no right to label me as mercenary just because your fiancée was! It just goes to prove how wrong we are for each other. You don't know the first thing about me."

"You don't understand me, either." Josh's voice was as cold as the night itself. "And it's clear you've never even tried. All right, maybe my judgment was a little clouded, but so is yours. You're still so busy resenting all men for what Mark did to your mother and your husband did to you that you don't have any energy left to love a man . . . any man! I do agree with you about one thing, though. We *are* wrong for each other. Completely wrong!"

Gears clashed, tires squealed and gravel rattled, violating the quiet stillness of the night. Otherwise, the remainder of the drive was accomplished in stony silence. When they reached Mark's house, Kitty went toward the door alone, too choked to speak even if she'd tried.

It would have been futile, anyway. Josh was already gone before she reached the steps.

Chapter Ten

While the man from the grocery store loaded the bags into the trunk of Mark's car, Kitty rubbed her hands together, wishing she'd remembered to bring her gloves. The sky was growing steadily darker, the air colder. A Texas blue norther was bearing down upon them.

When he'd closed the trunk, the man asked pleasantly, "You're Mark Winters's daughter, aren't you?"

Kitty smiled. "How'd you know?"

He shrugged. "Not many strangers in Rising Star, and people have been saying you were here. How's Mark getting along?"

"Very well," Kitty replied. "He's mainly irritated that the cast on his leg keeps him from being able to drive."

"Slows him down," the man said, grinning.

"Well, tell him Jake said hi, will you? I've missed him. We generally have some fine arguments about politics whenever he comes by."

"I'll tell him," Kitty promised. She got into the car and started it, then sat rubbing her icy hands while she waited for the motor to warm.

Everywhere she went, she met people who liked her father. The funny thing was that his popularity seemed to be in spite of, rather than because of, his fame as a movie actor. These people genuinely liked him for himself and they accepted him as one of them, a friend and a neighbor.

To be honest, she was liking him better every day herself. There was a warm, human side to Mark that was vastly appealing. Ever since he'd been home she'd been discovering things about him that continued to erode her long-held negative opinions. Mark was fun and witty and a good conversationalist, but he was much more than that. She was learning that he had a kind heart, a generous nature and a depth of thoughtfulness and compassion she would never have believed if she hadn't witnessed them herself. The day after he'd arrived home from the hospital, his housekeeper's son was injured on an oil rig in South Texas. Mark arranged for a small private plane to take her to him, in addition to paying all her expenses while she was there.

One night recently, he'd told her stories of his grandfather, who as a young man had gone to California to join the gold rush. When he was returning to Texas, his saddlebag full of gold, he'd narrowly escaped from a band of Indians as

his horse swam a river. Kitty had remarked that
it sounded like a John Wayne movie to her, and
Mark had grinned and agreed. "Maybe that's
why I took up acting, so I could pretend to have
as exciting a life as my grandfather really
did."

This past week and a half they had talked
about many things, but both of them had ginger-
ly skirted their personal relationship. Despite
Mark's touching speech the night of his homecoming party, despite Kitty's evident thawing,
there still remained a small measure of reserve
between them. Kitty sensed that Mark, though
warm and friendly, was holding back from any
further demonstrations of fatherly affection for
her sake. He didn't want to demand more than
she could give, and she appreciated that. She
knew he was determined not to make her feel
tied down or burdened.

Yet a burden lay heavily on her heart all the
same—the burden of her love for Josh. Kitty had
not felt able to confide in Mark about her feelings
for Josh. She didn't feel quite that close to him.
And besides, there was nothing Mark could have
done if he had known about it.

Over a week had gone by since the night she'd
last seen Josh, yet not a waking hour had passed
without her thinking of him. And each time she
did, Kitty's pain swelled afresh, raw and stinging.

She loved him . . . there was no getting
around that fact. And there was no getting
around the fact that in the time he'd been away,
there had been no softening in him, for the

silence had been piercingly loud. Not even Mark had received a phone call from Josh, an unusual departure from the norm that puzzled him more than it seemed to actually worry him.

Kitty had indeed gotten what she'd wished for—plenty of time for some plain thinking. Josh was gone, uncommunicative, and she missed him dreadfully. It was bad enough during the day whenever she thought of him—which was practically all the time—but nights were far worse. Alone in her bed, sleep constantly eluded her as she remembered the times in his arms and, most especially, that one gloriously rich evening when they'd made love.

She hated this senseless beating herself with such memories, but she could no more forget them than she could have stopped the norther that was gusting down from the Panhandle.

That day when they'd unexpectedly met each other and had lunch, Josh had teasingly suggested they might be falling in love. What, Kitty wondered now as she slowly drove out of town, would have happened if she'd told him she was already in love with him? Would they be together now or would her admission have scared him away? That very same night when she'd refused to go home with him, he had asked if she was holding out for a marriage offer. She shuddered, remembering that dangerous calm, knowing that the undercurrent of anger had been explosive. He'd felt she was playing games, trying to trap him into a commitment he didn't want to make.

But she feared such a commitment as much

as he did, perhaps more. She still remembered the bleak, dark months following her divorce. She couldn't—she simply couldn't—face such an ordeal ever again. Though Josh quite frankly didn't want to fall into that trap either, he did want a relationship, and Kitty was terrified of both. The level of emotional involvement they'd already attained was frightening enough. And the pain . . . the pain had already come.

Her head ached from the merry-go-round of thought; moreover, it got her precisely nowhere. When she neared a junction between a gravel road and the blacktop, impulsively she slowed and turned off. Maybe a short visit with Ellie would help pull her out of this melancholy mood. The groceries in back would be fine. On a freezing day like this, nothing was going to spoil if she delayed rushing home to the refrigerator.

Ellie met her at the door with a welcoming smile. "Come in, come in. Carol is here and we've been admiring my wedding dress. Want to see?"

"Of course I want to see it!" Kitty exclaimed. She followed Ellie down the hall and into her bedroom, where Carol was seated on the edge of the bed, admiring the dress spread across it.

The dress was exquisite, a champagne-colored lace dotted with tiny brown seed pearls. Satin shoes to match lay next to a small headpiece of flowers and pearls, again picking up the brown and champagne color scheme.

"It's gorgeous," Kitty said. "You're going to knock Dad's eyes out in that!"

Ellie's eyes twinkled. "That's the idea," she

laughed, "so you girls mustn't look too glamorous yourselves and outshine me."

"How about modeling for us?" Kitty asked.

Ellie laughed. "I thought you'd never ask. I—"

The telephone rang, and Ellie broke off to move around the bed to answer it. A brief moment passed and then a smile softened her lips. "Hi, darling. I love you, too." She sat down on the edge of the bed, then, remembering her guests, said, "Just a moment, Mark." She turned and suggested, "Carol, why don't you make some coffee? Kitty can help you."

Carol winked at Kitty. "Do you get the impression we're *de trop*?"

"Definitely." Kitty laughed. "My feelings are hurt. Aren't yours?"

As they left the room, Kitty discreetly closed the bedroom door. Once they were in the kitchen, Carol giggled. "All that gooey love talk! Seems kind of strange coming from people their age, doesn't it?"

Kitty shrugged. "Not to me. I've gone through it twice—first with Mom a couple of years ago, and now Mark. I'm beginning to wonder whether the only happy couples are the older ones."

"Not so," Carol stated firmly. "If last night is any indication"—she rolled her eyes provocatively—"I'd say Adam and I are *supremely* happy!"

Kitty laughed. "Okay, okay, point taken!" She sat down at the table. "By the way, where's little Adam today? I bought him a stuffed duck in town."

"He's asleep, thank heaven, in the other bedroom, and if you wake him up for a duck, I'll make turkey soup out of you."

They both laughed. Carol brought cups and saucers to the table, then paused to study Kitty with penetrating thoroughness. "Speaking of sleep, you don't look as though you've had much lately."

"You want to tuck *me* in for a nap, too?" Kitty asked crossly.

"If you keep snapping at me that way, I will," Carol said.

"Sorry." Kitty sighed. "Remember that ear you promised me?"

Carol nodded. "I'm listening."

"It . . . it's Josh," Kitty began.

"That much," Carol said dryly, "I'd already figured out for myself, especially since the night of Mark's homecoming party."

"Is it that obvious?" Kitty asked, dismayed.

"Maybe not to everyone," Carol answered, "but I could see the signs. Go ahead. What's wrong?"

Kitty grimaced. "I'm not sure I can explain it so that it makes any sense, because I don't understand it myself. Josh and I are . . . well, we're involved. And yet, we're not."

Carol frowned. "Either you are or you aren't."

"I told you it didn't make sense," Kitty said wryly. "We both care about each other. At least, I still care for him. I'm not sure how Josh feels right now. But I'm terrified of getting too serious. I had a really lousy marriage, Carol, and I swore to myself then that I'd never let myself get hurt like that again. Josh has made it perfectly clear he's against marriage too, but that doesn't stop him from wanting to have a serious relationship. He wants me to stay here, but to my way of thinking, all that would do is simply delay the painful day of parting."

"You're in love with him, aren't you?" Carol asked.

Kitty bowed her head. "Yes. Oh, yes, damn it, I am!"

"That's a fine state for someone who's unsure whether she's involved or not," Carol teased. Immediately she became serious again. "And Josh? Does he love you?"

Kitty shook her head. "Right now I think he actually hates me," she said sadly. "He did care before our last quarrel, but I don't think it was love. Oh, Carol, it's a hopeless situation. We're always arguing, always saying hateful things to each other, and then we . . ." Her lips trembled and her voice halted.

"Never mind," Carol said gently. "You know what I think? I think you ought to stop all the fighting and tell Josh how you really feel."

"So he can feel sorry for me?" Kitty asked miserably.

"Maybe he'll say he loves you too," Carol pointed out reasonably.

"It wouldn't make any difference," Kitty said. "We're all wrong for each other. People who can't get along don't belong together."

"The night of Mark's party, I saw both of you stealing glances at each other when you thought the other one wasn't looking, and I saw the expression in Josh's eyes. I think he loves you, Kitty, but he's been hurt in the past, just as you have. I saw Dana operate, and it would've been a miracle if he hadn't ended up being wary after her. She had an absolute genius for putting him down and making him feel worthless. Actually, I think he had a lucky break in not marrying her, but she managed to do an awful lot of damage to his ego before she dumped him. Now you've come along, and you're inheriting the fallout. Both of you have been scarred so badly, I don't think either of you is aware just how much you're hurting the other in your desperate attempts not to be hurt."

Kitty was thoughtful as she drove home a half hour later. Carol was right in some ways. Certainly she had been more preoccupied with her own fragile vulnerabilities than she'd been about what effect her attitude might have on Josh. Maybe it was the same with him . . . maybe he really was just as afraid as she was.

Not that it changed anything. Josh's silence all week told her plainly things between them were at an end. It was just as well. Neither of them knew how to trust anymore, and without trust, any relationship was doomed.

The weather began intruding on her thoughts. A strong wind whipped across the plains, blowing dust and whistling at the car windows, and the sky was an intense, angry blue. The air was growing colder by the moment, and Kitty turned the car's heater to full blast. By the time she reached the house, the first raindrops were falling. Kitty was grateful she'd made it home before the worst of the storm began.

Juggling her handbag and two bags of groceries, Kitty reached the kitchen door. Before she could turn the knob, the door swung open. Mark, on his crutches, leaned against the door to hold it open while she entered.

"I'm glad you're back," he said.

"Me, too." Kitty set her bags on the table. "It looks like we're in for a bad storm."

Mark closed the door and made his way awkwardly across the room. "We are," he agreed. "I've been listening to the weather reports and they're saying this will be a real blizzard. Red and Oakie have been at it all afternoon putting out extra rations in the pastures. They had my truck loaded with hay, all set to go over to Josh's place to do the same there, when Red ripped his hand on some barbed wire."

"Is he all right?" Kitty asked, concerned.

"I don't know. Oakie's taken him into town to see a doctor."

"What about Josh's cattle? Will Oakie be able to take care of them when he gets back?"

"I don't see how. This storm is coming on fast." Mark glanced toward the window with a worried frown. "Once that bridge of Josh's freezes over, nobody will be able to get in. I doubt Oakie'll make it back before that happens. I tried to reach Adam to see if he could do it, but I couldn't get him. I guess he's out tending to his own livestock. Damn this leg!" he snarled in frustration. "Here I am, helpless as a baby when I'm really needed."

"Does it make that much difference?" Kitty asked quietly. "I mean, can't one of the men just go in the morning?"

Mark shook his head. "There'd still be the problem with the bridge. And if we get a hard freeze, Oakie will have his hands full chopping ice on the water tanks and burning the prickly pear so the cattle can get enough fluids. With Red and me both out of action, he'll be overworked as it is."

"Then I'll go," Kitty said decisively.

Mark shook his head again. "No, honey. It's good of you to offer, but if you went over there now, you might get stuck on account of the bridge. You wouldn't be able to get back home, and there'd be nobody around to help you."

"I'll be fine," Kitty assured him. "And if the bridge freezes over before I can get out, I'll just sleep at Josh's house. In fact, that's probably best anyway. That way I can get back into his pastures in the morning to break the ice on his tanks."

"You sure you don't mind?" Mark's gaze was admiring. "It would be a tremendous help. I'm responsible for Josh's livestock when he's away on my business, and I've been worrying myself crazy trying to figure out how to do it."

"Of course I don't mind," Kitty said, sounding braver than she actually felt.

Thirty minutes later she drove through the gate onto Josh's property. Once again she held her breath as she crossed the narrow bridge. She drove past the house and barn and straight toward the first pasture gate. Struggling with the unfamiliar keys, she felt the wind cut through her like a knife. Her rain slicker and wool scarf flapped wildly, and the frigid rain chilled her through her clothing.

Because it would soon be totally dark, Kitty worked at a feverish pace, dreading being caught by nightfall in the unfamiliar terrain. She was all too conscious of the dangers to her if she were. It would be fatally easy to take a wrong turn or get stuck in the mud or go blindly down an unseen gully.

By the time she'd gone through the second gate, the rain was turning to sleet. Kitty nibbled nervously at her lips as she clambered from the warmth of the truck into the raw elements. She climbed into the back of the truck, where she struggled to topple a bale of hay over the side. Then it was back into the cab again and on to the next stop.

She pitied the poor cattle that came crowding around the truck at every stop she made, bawling unhappily at her, but beyond dropping the hay for them, she had no time to waste on sympathy. She was fighting that swiftly falling darkness, fighting her own growing alarm that she might yet get stuck out there, for the sleet was making the driving more treacherous every moment.

Josh gritted his teeth as he drove across the narrow bridge. The sleet had already made the road slippery and the bridge was dangerous. But he made it safely across and expelled a breath of relief.

As soon as he pulled up before the garage, he saw the twin beams of headlights off in the west pasture. Red and Oakie must be putting out feed, he decided, but what puzzled him was why they'd waited until dark to do it.

Josh was exhausted. He'd been up early for a business meeting before rushing to the L.A. airport to catch his flight to Dallas. He'd originally planned to stay there overnight. There was an office complex for sale, and he'd intended to look it over the next morning. But when he'd heard the weather reports, he'd decided to come home at once. If the storm was as severe as it was predicted to be, Mark's ranch hands would have all the work they could handle on the Winters ranch without having to worry about his place too.

But he hadn't expected to have to go to work the minute he arrived home. Tired as he was, Josh drove around to the barn, threw several bales of hay into the back of his truck and set out across the pastures to help.

When he approached the other truck, he was astounded as his headlights picked out the slim figure wrestling a bale of hay up to the edge of the truck bed. It tipped over the side, and only then did Kitty turn and look toward the lights.

"Oakie, is that you?" she called out. "That was my last bale."

Josh got out and walked toward her, stepping into the light so that Kitty could recognize him.

"No, it's me," he said unnecessarily as he watched her swing over the tailgate to the ground. "What're you doing out here?" he asked.

"Killing time, of course," she answered saucily. "What else?"

Josh grinned at her. It was all he could do to keep from sweeping her into his arms. He'd thought of her night and day for the past ten days, loving her, hating her, wanting her, being furious with her, and now here she was. This lovely creature who belonged in designer gowns at glittering parties, cool as you please, was tending to a herd of hungry, miserable cattle on a freezing night. What a paradox she was!

"Mind if I hang around and help?" he asked. "I don't have anything better to do either. And besides, I brought a load of hay."

"Good." Kitty sighed, betraying her exhaustion. "I didn't think I'd have the energy to go back to the barn and load more, much less the willpower to make myself come out here again. We've still got the south and far west pastures to do."

Josh nodded. "We'll leave your truck and pick it up on the way back." He opened the door of Mark's truck, cut the motor and turned off the lights.

While Kitty drove, Josh rode in the back, tossing out the hay and hopping to the ground periodically to open and close gates. It was a much more efficient system than working alone, and they finished the task much sooner than she'd believed possible.

Finally Josh climbed into the heated cab beside her. His clothes were soaked, and he shivered as he leaned toward the heater's vents, rubbing his hands. "Home, James," he said lightly. "I need a hot bath and so do you."

"And some hot coffee," Kitty said dreamily.

"And some hot soup," Josh suggested. "Or chili."

"Even better," Kitty said approvingly. "And," she added to the menu, "let's not forget that wonderful invention, the hot toddy."

"Hmmmmm." Josh smiled. "And hot flames in the fireplace."

"Absolutely."

"Do you think we're a little giddy?" Josh asked.

"I'm a lot giddy," Kitty said. "Now that you're here."

Josh whistled softly. "I'm flattered."

Kitty chuckled, but she swallowed it quickly as the truck lurched through a pothole. She clutched the steering wheel tighter and said, "I'd have been drunk with joy at the sight of the devil himself as long as it meant I wasn't out here alone anymore. I had terrifying visions of getting stuck, or lost in the darkness, and freezing to death."

"I guess I've been put in my place," Josh said, amused. "And here I was hoping you'd missed me."

They'd reached Mark's truck again, and Kitty shifted into neutral. For a long moment she stared straight ahead, but finally she turned toward him.

"I did," she said simply.

Josh caught his breath and reached for her, but he only grasped the air. Kitty had opened the door and slipped out.

Chapter Eleven

The strong north wind tossed icy daggers of sleet against the roof and windows of the house. Josh closed the door against the vicious storm and then looked at Kitty. She was removing the dripping rain slicker, and the coat and jeans she wore beneath were damp, too. Raindrops and tiny slivers of ice dusted her hair with silver.

Josh brushed his hand through it, dislodging the pellets of ice, and Kitty's eyes widened. She looked startled, almost fearful, like a doe surprised by a hunter. He dropped his hand and turned his back to her; the realization that Kitty was afraid of him was crushing.

"Go get your bath," he said gruffly as he shed his own soggy coat. "You're chilled."

"I'll just change my clothes," Kitty answered. "I can wait until I get home to bathe."

Josh whipped around. "You're not going," he stated. "It's too dangerous. The bridge and highway are already slick. You must have planned to stay, anyway," he added, nodding toward the small overnight case she'd brought in from the truck, "or you wouldn't have brought that along."

"Only so I could check on the cattle and the water tanks in the morning. But now that you're home, I'm not needed."

Not needed! If only she knew, Josh groaned inwardly, then thrust the disturbing thought away and dealt with the matter at hand. "What if you had an accident on the way? You might not even be found until morning. I can't let you go, Kitty. If anything were to happen to you, I . . . I . . ."

His voice trailed off and Kitty swallowed over the lump in her throat. The undisguised anguish in his voice elated her. He did still care! Her mind clung to the thought as though it were a life raft. Josh cared!

Yet a wide gulf still yawned between them, a gulf that was essential to preserve, for both their sakes. All the same, she realized he was right about how foolhardy it would be to attempt to cross the ice-slick bridge in the darkness, not to mention slithering along several miles of highway that wound through dark countryside. The idea was no more comforting than her earlier fear of being stuck all night in a storm-ravaged pasture.

But if she was to stay, she had to set the tone . . . an impersonal tone for the rest of the evening. They were too isolated here, the situation too intimate. They would have to take extreme care to behave as any two people might who'd suddenly been thrown together for a night because of an emergency . . . polite and agreeable, but no more. Otherwise . . . otherwise . . .

"All right," she said briskly. "I'll stay, but you'll take the first bath because you're more soaked than I am."

Josh understood the game plan. They were to be civil yet distant, with their guards up. He nodded and, masking a chill that suddenly went through him, went toward the telephone. "Let's see if this is working. You ought to call Mark and . . ." He lifted the receiver and, frowning, replaced it a second later. "I was afraid of that. The lines are down."

"Surely Mark won't worry; he expected me to stay," Kitty reasoned. Still, she would have felt better if she could have spoken to him. She honestly didn't want him to be anxious on her behalf, but it seemed it couldn't be helped.

Her own anxiety at the moment, however, was for Josh. She hadn't missed the convulsive shiver that had raced through him, though he'd tried to hide it from her. Now her gaze was critical as it swept over him. His shirt was plastered to his skin, and his slacks were saturated and muddy. His hair fell limp and damp against his forehead. He looked tired; the strain of traveling and working long hours showed in his face.

"Go get that bath," she ordered quietly.

Two hours later they had finally thawed out. First there had been coffee and hot baths, followed by steaming bowls of soup. Now a lovely fire blazed in the living room and, nursing drinks, each of them dressed in a robe, they sat on large floor pillows before the fireplace.

They had worked hard to get past the intimacy of their circumstances by talking of safe, impersonal topics. Josh discussed his trip with her, explaining some of the finer points of Mark's business dealings, while Kitty told him about the wedding plans that were under way. They both laughed as she humorously described some of the crises that kept cropping up.

"I thought it was supposed to be a simple affair," Josh said.

"It was." Kitty shook her head. "But I'm not sure Mark even *knows* how to do anything simple. I suppose it's a throwback to all those years in Hollywood. He's already drawn up a guest list of three hundred."

Josh looked thunderstruck. "To fit in Ellie's *house?*" he asked incredulously.

"They compromised after a few million arguments," Kitty explained. "The ceremony will take place in her house with only the immediate family and about a dozen close friends. The rest of the guests will attend the elaborate reception at the club with a formal dinner and dance. You know, of course, that you're to be his best man, don't you?"

Josh nodded, then asked in amusement, "What about the honeymoon? Has Mark booked a flight to the moon?"

Kitty's eyes twinkled with glee. "Oh, the honeymoon's a whole different battle, and it's still raging, as far as I know. Mark wants to take Ellie on a three-month trip around the world. She thinks three days on South Padre Island ought to do it."

Josh laughed heartily and Kitty's heart lurched. He looked so happy and relaxed; she thought she'd never seen him more handsome. Or more disturbing. She was already far more aware of him than was good for her. He wore a deep burgundy velour robe with pale blue pajama pants beneath, but he obviously wasn't wearing the shirt because she had a mind-shattering view of his chest where the robe gaped open. The sight of dark golden skin and wiry black chest hair sent tingles along her spine, and though she tried her best not to notice, again and again her gaze was drawn to that enticing spot. Now she forced herself to look at his face as he laughed, but that turned out to be no easier on her already unsettled heart. The skin around his eyes had crinkled into tiny wings, and his smile—well, no other man could possibly have a better one, she thought, with such well-shaped lips and white, even teeth. It transformed his whole face, and she found herself breathless as she fought the urge to touch it.

She looked into the leaping flames in the fireplace and reminded herself to be sensible. There was always a tomorrow to be reckoned with. Moreover, her thoughts trooped on grimly, it was quite apparent Josh didn't share her chaotic feelings. For the past half-hour they'd sat near enough that they could have reached out and touched each other, yet he seemed oblivious to her. Whatever interest he'd once had in her had clearly vanished during the days he'd been away.

Kitty had no idea how much of a strain it was on Josh to simulate indifference to her. Here she was, isolated with him from the rest of the world on a savagely stormy night, wearing only that attractive blue robe over a white gown that now and again peeked through at her knees, looking utterly beautiful and desirable. His entire body ached for her, and it took every ounce of self-restraint he possessed to keep from touching her. If he did, even once, he knew he would lose all control. The last evening they'd spent together she'd rejected him, and tonight would be no different—except for one thing. Tonight she had to stay here, and it would be intolerably awkward for them both if a fresh constraint rose between them.

He glared fiercely into his glass. He rarely drank and always sparingly, but tonight he thought it wouldn't be such a bad idea to get smashed. Maybe it would help him to stop thinking about her, to stop wanting her. If nothing else it would give him something to do with his hands and his lips.

Josh got to his feet and said, "Give me your glass. I'll make you another drink."

Kitty didn't look at him as she shook her head. "No, thanks. It doesn't take much alcohol to give me a splitting headache."

Josh sighed and set his own glass on the lamp table. "I don't really want another one either," he admitted. "What I want . . . is you."

Kitty tilted her head to look up at him, then closed her eyes and sighed. "Oh, Josh," she said weakly. "Oh, Josh."

Her face, washed clean of makeup, was beautiful in its purity. Firelight cast copper and gold through the thick tresses of her hair. Josh longed to run his fingers through it, but he kept still, angry at giving himself away when he'd been so determined to say nothing, to do nothing. Kitty's eyes remained closed, her silent message unmistakable. She was saying no again, loud and clear.

Josh swallowed, and turned away. "It's all right," he said, keeping his voice as casual as he could manage. "You're perfectly safe. I don't intend to bother you with any unwanted attentions when you can't run away from me."

Kitty opened her eyes, shocked at the inflection of pain she'd recognized in his voice. Josh's back was to her, and he took a step away as though he were about to leave the room. All at once she knew she couldn't let this moment end. Tomorrow she could be sensible again; tonight . . . tonight she yearned to be a woman once more.

She scrambled to her feet and choked out,

"Josh! Josh, please." He stopped, but did not turn, and Kitty saw with dismay that his shoulders and back were taut. She'd waited too long. Or had she? She licked her dry lips and tried again. "Please?"

Josh finally turned. His gray eyes were hooded, his jaw set. "Please what?" he grated. "Pretend I never said that? Pretend I don't want you?"

Kitty moved toward him quickly and her fingers closed around the lapels of his robe. Unable to meet his gaze, she stared at her unsteady hands. "Please," she began huskily. "I . . . I want you, too."

A stunned silence followed. There was only the sound of the crackling fire behind them, the howling wind and the clattering sleet outside. "What exactly," Josh finally asked in a cautious voice, "are you saying?"

"That . . ." Kitty paused and nibbled at her lip. "That I want you tonight, Josh. I want . . ." Here her voice grew lower until it was but a whisper. "I want you to hold me and kiss me and make love to me."

Josh groaned, and when he opened his arms Kitty stepped into them, savoring their hard strength, the warmth of being snuggled to his chest.

"You're driving me mad, you know that, don't you?" he murmured against her soft hair. "Ever since that one night together you're all I think about, but you keep me in such a state of uncertainty. You want me; then you don't. Now you do again. But why, Kitty? Why have you changed

your mind since that last night we were together?"

Kitty shook her head. "Ask me something I
know the answer to," she said faintly. "I've been
trying so hard for both our sakes to stay aloof, to
keep a safe distance, but it isn't working. I can't
let go of you."

He gently tipped back her head, forcing her to
look into his eyes. "We've been trying so hard to
keep ourselves from hurting that that's all we've
managed to accomplish," he said seriously.

"I know," Kitty whispered. His lips were tan-
talizingly close. "I know."

They kissed and a fireball of passion exploded
between them. Instantly they were both alight,
their blood leaping hotly and their flesh burning
with desire. Josh's hands at Kitty's shoulders
had been gentle for one brief moment, but now
one hand went to the nape of her neck, pressing
her closer, while his other slid between the folds
of her robe.

Josh's lips were soft, yet ruthless in their
demands. Kitty yielded completely to the sensual insistence, parting her lips so that his tongue
could find hers, igniting still more flames within her. She arched toward him, naturally, instinctively, as his hand stroked her back and
hips.

Her own fingers sneaked beneath the lapels of
his robe, gently fanning across his bare, warm
chest, and the action seemed to electrify him.
Lifting his mouth from hers, Josh looked deeply
into her eyes, passion glittering in his own like
sunlight on silver. Then he bent, wrapping one

arm around her back, another behind her knees, and he lowered her gently to the rug.

Slowly, as though there were all the time in the world, they undressed each other, pausing often to kiss or caress and to smile. Despite the icy storm that screamed outside the windows, they were both warmed—by flesh touching flesh, and by the fire in the hearth, which seemed to become part of them. Its light illuminated and concealed, licking, flickering, alternately casting shadows and golden beams across their shimmering bodies.

Kitty was dazzled by the soft pale sheen across Josh's shoulders and chest, by the blue shadows that fell over the planes of his face and lent mysterious depths to his eyes. She reveled in the clean scent of his skin and the heat that his body radiated. Her heart raced as her fingertips traveled across smooth curves, sharp angles, hard muscles, the crisp hair of his chest. She was enthralled by the power of his body, convinced now that it was for the joy of being in this man's arms, of touching him and being touched by him, for the experience of being made whole and complete by him, that she had been born. She sighed softly, relinquishing mind and body and thought to the rightness of it.

The mingling sounds of howling wind and snapping fire and their own raspy breathing gave Josh a sense of primitive oneness with the storm and with this woman. With rising passion, he made love to every inch of her. As he kissed the thrusting peaks of her breasts, or stroked her tender, smooth thighs, his own ecstasy thundered louder, responding to the wild frenzy that ruled Kitty. They became two natural creatures —elemental, basic, true to their inborn instincts. It became a mating that was direct and honest, for there was only the truth between them—a truth so rare it was exquisitely, almost unearthly beautiful.

They came together as naturally as they breathed, flowing together into a river of completion. A wave crashed and the strong currents tossed them up, lifting them to the heights of exultation. The foaming waters of life and loving, of enhancing another being while being enhanced, burst forth in a shower of magnificent splendor, powerful, intense, inexorable and utterly consuming.

Josh held Kitty close, so close he could feel her heart thudding in that final moment of bliss, and for a long time afterward he simply held her. She was a part of him, heart and soul, and he wanted to go on holding her forever.

Kitty, too, was reluctant to draw away. She seemed to be floating somewhere outside herself in a place where supreme contentment was law, where there was only happiness and satisfaction. At the same time she was still flesh and blood, aware of the joy of being enveloped by the warmth of Josh. Her arms clung to him, holding him tight, as she buried her face beneath his chin, pressing her cheek to his moist chest.

"I've never been this happy before," she admitted recklessly. "Never." Her hand traced a circle across his back.

Josh stroked her shoulder, and she felt his lips

press lightly against it before he sighed, "Neither have I." He lifted his head to look into her eyes and his smile was tender. "You know we're going to have to resolve this thing somehow, don't you? Our feelings for each other keep getting more intense instead of less."

Kitty's hand stilled. "Yes," she said after a moment. "I suppose so. But not now. I don't want to think about that now."

"Why not?" Josh asked gruffly. He pulled away from her and rolled over to his side. "We've got to think about it, talk about it. You can't just get on a plane after Mark's wedding and go back to Chicago as though all this hasn't happened . . . can you?" His eyes darkened as he waited.

Kitty was chilled now that his body no longer shielded hers, but his words sent shivers along her spine that had nothing at all to do with the cold night. She sat up and reached for her discarded robe. "Why are you doing this?" she demanded. "Why are you spoiling everything now?" Her voice caught on a sob of frustration.

"I'm not trying to spoil anything," Josh snapped. He picked up his own robe and shrugged into it. "All I'm trying to do is come to some sensible solution about us, but all you want to do is bury your head in the sand. What are we going to do? Nothing? Just have a little fling and call it quits with no looking back? Can you do that, Kitty?"

"I don't know!" she cried. "I don't know! What do you want me to say? That I'll stay here indefinitely and have an on-again, off-again affair with you—whenever we happen not to be fighting, that is? Damn it, Josh, I don't know what you expect me to say!"

Josh heaved a deep breath. "Neither do I," he said in a more reasonable tone. He stared down into the fire. "Maybe I just want you to tell me honestly that you care, to at least admit that what's going on between us has some importance beyond the moment, that it warrants a bit of consideration before you just toss it all away."

"All right, all right!" Kitty was no longer reasonable at all. Defensive and angry, her voice was shrill. "I care. I care a lot. Is that what you want to hear? But that doesn't change anything. You're just as paranoid about getting serious as I am! We're both too suspicious, too afraid, too quick to argue. I can't see anything but trouble ahead between us, and who needs it? Who needs it?" Her voice broke again and she turned her back to him, burying her face in her hands.

Josh went cold all over. He thrust his knotted fists into the pockets of his robe, and his eyes were hard and emotionless as he watched her sink to her knees before the fire. The tenderness he'd felt earlier was gone.

"For a little while, I thought I needed you," he said in a flat voice. "But I was wrong and you're right. Who needs it? What I need, you could never give."

Chapter Twelve

It was the intense cold that awakened her. Kitty opened her eyes and found the bedroom gray in the partial morning light. The air was frosty as she breathed. There was no heat in the house.

She shivered, dreading the instant when she had to leave what warmth there was beneath the covers. When she did at last, she dressed as hastily as her unsteady fingers would allow.

The house was in complete silence and Kitty wondered whether Josh was still asleep. The pain of the night came back to assault her as she slipped a heavy wool sweater over her head. There'd been the lovemaking—so glorious, so wonderful and fulfilling—followed by the dreadful quarrel, and after that the sharp tension of sharing the same close quarters without speaking except when strictly necessary.

The evening had ended with Kitty going to bed alone in Josh's room while he bunked on the living room sofa. There she had lain awake for hours, brushing away the tears that persisted in filling her eyes, longing for Josh, wishing he would come to her and end the intolerable distance that had come between them, yet knowing that he wouldn't.

Now, besides being cold, Kitty felt dull and achy from the tears she'd shed the night before. She crossed the room and opened the door quietly so that she wouldn't wake Josh. She went into the bathroom and flipped the light switch, and only then realized why there was no heat. The electricity was off. The butane tank was useless without the electric fans in the furnace.

She washed sparingly in the icy water and then headed toward the kitchen. When she passed through the living room, she saw that Josh wasn't, as she'd supposed, still asleep. There were discarded blankets piled haphazardly at one end of the sofa, and cold, dead ashes in the fireplace.

In the kitchen she found his brief note: "A power line snapped during the night—no electricity or heat, but you can use the kitchen stove because it's gas. I've gone to check on the cattle. Don't try to leave until I have a chance to sand the bridge."

Kitty sighed. There was no salutation, no signature—only the stark message. But then, she asked herself angrily, what had she expected . . . a love letter?

Mentally shaking herself, she tossed away the note and then busied herself. She put some water on to boil for coffee and lit all the other burners on the stove as well. While she waited for the water, she decided to build a fire in the fireplace, but the woodbox beside it was nearly empty. They'd used most of the firewood last night. She would have to bring in a supply.

Kitty slipped on her coat, wrapped her wool scarf about her head and went out the back door, and there she paused to catch her breath. Everything was pristine white—the wide stretch of pastures, the garage roof, the tops of the fence posts, the tree branches. She was entranced; the snow seemed so different from the dirty slush in the city. This was beautiful and clean, giving the landscape a gentle serenity after the storm of the night.

The leaden gray of the sky contrasted sharply with the white frosted earth, and the air was still and calm. Later, she thought, there would be more snow.

The penetrating cold reminded Kitty of her task. She hurried to the woodpile beside the garage, brushed away the snow that covered it and trudged back to the house carrying a load of firewood in her arms.

Inside, she found the water boiling, so she dumped the wood beside the fireplace and went back to make her coffee. After that she coaxed a fire into being.

A half-hour later the temperature in the living room and kitchen was tolerable. Kitty had shut the hall door leading to the rest of the house so that what warmth there was would remain in the two rooms. She huddled close to the fireplace as she sipped a cup of coffee and, for the first time that morning, began to feel comfortable.

Poor Josh, though, must be half-frozen out there in the pastures. She wondered whether she ought to go out and try to help him. But on the heels of the thought came a frightened reluctance. He might still be so angry that he would resent her presence.

In the end she decided it was best to do what she could in the house. She tidied the living room, stored away the blankets Josh had used during the night, then straightened up the bedroom and bath. After that, she raided his freezer and pantry.

By midmorning, she was pleased with her accomplishments. On the stove, a hearty beef stew simmered; a pecan pie was baking in the oven, and some muffins were cooling on the counter.

At eleven-thirty she made a fresh pot of coffee, just in case. She had no way of knowing when Josh would return, but since there hadn't been any evidence that he'd eaten breakfast before he left the house, she felt sure he would be starving when he did arrive. If he wasn't back by one, she would load the food in Mark's truck and go in search of him.

She waited somewhat impatiently for him, and suddenly it struck her as ridiculously ironic

that she, who had become so fiercely independent since her divorce, was suddenly behaving
like a wife. She'd cleaned Josh's house, cooked
Josh's meal, and now she eagerly awaited his
return home. Not only was it ridiculous and
ironic, it was also somewhat frightening.

What was it she did want? she asked herself
dismally. And what did Josh want? Physically
they were undeniably compatible, but there had
to be more to a relationship than that if it was to
endure over time. She was determined not to
make a second mistake with her life by choosing
the wrong man again. She loved Josh; certainly
whenever she was in his arms it *felt* right, but
did that *make* it right? Even Josh seemed ambivalent. He wanted her to stay, but he, too, was
unwilling to put a name to his feelings or make
any sort of commitment.

It was twelve-thirty when Josh entered the
house, and he looked exhausted. The lower part
of his face was dark with an overnight growth of
beard, but what alarmed Kitty was that the rest
of his face had a grayish cast to it. As he shed his
coat and hat, his entire demeanor was one of a
man worn out almost to the point of dropping.
Before he could speak, he began to cough.

"Are you all right?" Kitty's anxious eyes
searched his face.

"I'm fine," Josh said. "Just tired, that's all."
He rubbed his hands together. "Lord, but it's
cold out there."

"Go sit in the living room," Kitty said. "There's
a fire and I'll bring you some coffee."

"That sounds great." Josh inhaled deeply and

almost, but not quite, smiled. "What's that smell?"

"Stew, pecan pie and muffins." Kitty crossed the room to the stove and poured two cups of coffee. "I didn't think you'd mind if I commandeered your kitchen."

"Not at all. I'm grateful. I don't think I have enough energy left to open a can of beans." They went into the living room, where Josh lowered himself wearily to the sofa and stretched out his long legs toward the fire.

Kitty sank to one of the floor cushions near the fire, and after Josh had taken a couple of sips of coffee, she ventured, "How did the cattle fare last night?"

Josh gave his head a negative shake and said grimly, "Not good. I found one cow and two calves dead, and the rest of them look numb and half-gone."

"I'm sorry," Kitty murmured.

"So am I," Josh answered. "Damned sorry. I even found one of them dead on top of the ice on the tank. Broken limbs, I guess." He shrugged as though trying to put the horror of it away from him and drained his cup. "Is there enough for a refill?"

"Of course." Kitty got to her feet.

Because it was warmer by the fire, and Josh looked too exhausted to move anyway, Kitty brought their plates into the living room a while later. She'd only been gone a short time, but when she returned, she found Josh with his eyes closed.

"Josh?" she asked softly.

The dark eyelashes swept up. "Ummmm?" He sat up and smiled sleepily. "I must have dozed off."

"Maybe I should have just let you sleep."

"No. I'd rather eat. Thanks," he added as she set his plate in front of him on the coffee table.

Kitty took her place at the opposite end of the sofa, and at that moment Josh went into a severe coughing spasm. It sounded awful, as though it came from deep in his chest.

When it ended, he reached for his glass of water and drained it.

"Your cough is getting worse by the minute!" Kitty exclaimed. "Is there any cough medicine in the house?"

Josh shook his head. "No," he gasped, coughing again. "But I'll be all right."

"I'm not so sure," Kitty said. "You must have taken a chill last night when you got so wet, and working outside in the cold this morning has just aggravated it. You ought to be in bed. You need rest."

"I told you, I'm fine," Josh snapped. "And I sure don't need you playing mother hen!" He picked up his fork.

"I wasn't!" His words had frozen her like a cold north wind. "But I am concerned about you."

"Well, don't be! The last thing I need is for you to be hovering over me and acting worried just like a . . . just like a wife, for God's sake! Just leave me alone, understand?"

"Yes," Kitty replied stiffly. "I understand perfectly." She stared down at her plate of food, but she knew she couldn't eat. A lump had closed her throat. Her concern had been genuine and spontaneous; she hadn't expected Josh's furious reaction. She felt a sudden need to get away from him. "I . . . I forgot the salt and pepper," she murmured as she started to get up.

There was a loud clatter as Josh dropped his fork to his plate. He grabbed Kitty's arm and pulled her down beside him again. "Damn it, I never seem to do anything right where you're involved. I didn't mean to hurt you." His voice was bleak.

"You didn't." Kitty averted her face, fighting the tears that threatened to spill from her eyes. "I was interfering and—"

"Stop it!" Josh commanded. He coughed again, then cleared his throat. "It's just no good, Kitty," he said at last.

"What isn't?"

"This. Us. The way things are. It's intolerable for both of us." He sighed raggedly. "I've been acting like a jerk, I know, but I can't seem to help myself. It's easier, I guess, than loving you."

Kitty's hand fluttered to her throat. "What," she asked unsteadily, "did you say?"

Josh rose and went to the window. "What does it matter?" he said expressionlessly.

"It matters a lot," Kitty breathed. Wild elation surged through her. This was the first time Josh had ever put into words what she'd been feeling. Now she at last felt she had come home. Now she could finally let go of the past, step forward and take a chance on the future. She got to her feet and went toward him. "Josh," she began softly, "I . . ."

He turned, and there was no responding warmth in his eyes, no loverlike tenderness in his face. Something in his gaze immediately placed a wall between them.

"I was awake half the night thinking," he said, "and you were right all along. Nothing can come of this insanity." He rubbed a hand across his forehead. "It's been a mad, impossible attraction from the beginning. We're from two separate worlds and there's no escaping that fact no matter what else is right or wrong between us. You're a city person; I'm a country man. We can never fit into each other's lives."

Kitty bridled. "You're telling me," she demanded indignantly, "I wouldn't fit in here, in your world?" At his nod, she flared, "Damn you, Joshua Steele! How many other women do you know who would've gone out in that storm last night to feed your cattle? Talk about a colossal nerve! You beat them all!"

"I didn't mean it like that," Josh explained patiently. "You were magnificent. No one can question that you've got grit, that you're a real trooper. But let's face it, Kitty. You weren't raised for this kind of life. You're meant for finer things, for all the nice modern conveniences of city living, for pretty clothes and fancy parties, not for this!" His hand swept around. "Life on a ranch can be tough. If there's not a drought, there's a hard freeze like this one. If your cattle don't die of that, they're liable to get killed off by disease. If that doesn't get them, then there's a glut on the market and you end up in the hole. Even when you can manage to squeeze out a profit, there's always the worry about next year and the year after. It's still a good life to those of us who love the wide open spaces, but it can be a lonely, hard one, too. I can't . . . I won't ask you," he said flatly, turning to look out the window once more, "to share the hardships of too much work and too little money. You'd only end up hating me."

There was a tiny silence. "In other words," Kitty said at last, "you're saying you don't want to marry me."

"I'm saying I *won't* marry you."

"Semantics," she snapped impatiently.

"No, there's a difference. I want you, but I intend to do what's best."

"Don't you think you're being unfair to me?"

He turned and stared at her. "Unfair? How?"

Kitty swallowed. "You're making a decision that concerns both of us without giving me a chance to participate. It affects my future as much as it does yours."

Josh shrugged. "Not really. You've said all along you intended to go back to Chicago, so why should I make a fool of myself by asking you to marry me just to give you the pleasure of refusing?"

"And what if I didn't?"

Josh laughed grimly and shook his head. "You're not catching me in that little trap. I'm not in the mood for 'what-if' games. Besides, even if you did want to marry me, I've just told you it wouldn't work out. I saw how miserable my parents' marriage was, and since then I've seen Mark's wife walk out on him and my own fiancée throw in the towel. This sort of life takes a special breed, a certain kind of toughness that you almost have to be born with. So let's not kid ourselves, okay? It just isn't for you, any more than city living would suit me."

"Fine," Kitty snapped. She felt so hurt, so betrayed, that all she could think of was to lash out and hurt him back as much as he'd just hurt her. "You're absolutely right! I *would* turn you down if you proposed to me. Flat! There's no way in this world I'd even dream of marrying a man who thinks that all I am is a shallow, light-weight character who can't cope!"

"Kitty, listen—"

"No!" she exclaimed hotly. "I've heard enough already from you! How *dare* you presume to judge me! Who gave you that right? You've made up your mind that I'm a fine play-thing, but not worth marrying! Well, I hate you for that, Josh, and I don't think I can ever forgive you!"

Josh paled. "You're wrong!" he said swiftly. His voice was filled with anguish. "I didn't mean it like that. You know I didn't."

"No, I don't," Kitty said sadly, her anger suddenly spent. "But it doesn't matter anymore. Nothing matters anymore." She tossed her head in proud defiance. "Would you mind doing me a favor and see whether the bridge is safe to cross, while I get my things together? I'd like to leave now."

Chapter Thirteen

"What is it, Kitten?" Mark asked over dinner. "Your mind is a thousand miles away."

Dinner had been spent in almost complete silence, but Kitty hadn't even realized it. Nor had she realized until Mark jolted her back to the present, that she'd scarcely touched her food.

But then, that seemed to be the norm today— preparing meals she didn't eat, performing chores she hardly recalled doing, moving and speaking and working in a vacuum of despair. She had barely even cared when the electricity came back on late in the afternoon.

The knowledge that Josh loved her had been magnificent for one brief moment—before he'd killed all hope, all joy. He'd been so implacable that she hadn't dared say she loved him, too.

Now she was glad she hadn't. It was easier this way; at least she still retained a tiny degree of her pride.

It was ironic how things worked out. She'd been the one who was reluctant to commit herself, to give their relationship a chance to grow into something important; yet when she was ready to alter that, Josh was the one who'd backed away. For so long she'd held on to her fears, terrified to let go and really feel, to be vulnerable, to love again, but bit by bit, without her being quite aware of it, Josh had undermined all that, stealing away the fears and doubts and replacing them with a growing confidence. She had dared once more to believe in a man, to trust him, to feel herself worthy of love, and the precise moment she did, he'd destroyed her.

"Kitten?"

Kitty looked across the table at her father. Concern was evident in his gentle gaze, and that was her undoing. She blinked hard and said tremulously, "Dad . . . I hate to disappoint you, but I . . . I just don't see how I can stay until your wedding, after all."

Mark didn't immediately try to change her mind as she'd expected. His blue eyes were thoughtful and knowing, and he amazed her by saying the one name that was inscribed in her heart and mind: "Josh."

Kitty's eyes widened. "How did you know?"

Mark smiled wryly. "Only my leg is broken, sweetheart, not my eyesight. I've watched the two of you ever since the first day you arrived in

Dallas. You're in love, but somehow it's gone wrong and now you're hurting."

"That about sums it up," Kitty said, fighting to keep her voice steady. "I . . . I really need to get away. I don't want to hurt your feelings, or Ellie's. This has nothing to do with either of you. But it's just no good for me here anymore."

Mark reached across the table and clasped her hand. "I'd be lying if I said I wasn't disappointed, Kitten, and I know Ellie will be too. But I understand. The last thing I ever wanted was for you to be hurt like this. I feel it's partly my fault."

Kitty shook her head. "Don't start trying to take on guilt that isn't yours."

"I can't help it." Mark shrugged. "If you hadn't come to see me, you wouldn't be suffering right now."

"No matter how other things have turned out," Kitty said, "I'll never be sorry I came." She managed a smile. "After all, I do have one thing I always wanted: my father."

"Have you really forgiven me," Mark asked wistfully, "for all those years I wasn't there?"

Kitty nodded. "I guess I've grown up a lot since coming here. What's the point of looking back when we can look ahead instead? If nothing else," she added unsteadily, "Josh did me a favor by pointing that out."

Mark's hand tightened over hers. "Then you're a lot more mature than me, because I can't help looking back and hating myself for all the years we missed together. You want to hear a confession, Kitten? Those early years, when you were still just a baby, I stayed away because you were so little. What did I know about baby girls? If I had spent weekends or holidays with you, I wouldn't have known what to do with you. And then time passed and you started to grow up. You were becoming a real person in your own right, with likes and dislikes and opinions and a personality, and I realized I didn't know the first thing about you and so that scared me off. What could we do together? What could we talk about? And of course, the older you got, the more the problem compounded. It was one thing to talk to you for five or ten minutes on the telephone once in a while, but quite another to spend time with the lovely young lady in the photographs you sent me. She was just a beautiful stranger who happened to bear my name." He removed his hand from hers and no longer met her eyes. "I think what was wrong with all my close relationships was that I was afraid to let people really get to know me . . . the real me. I was afraid if they did, they'd find out I was nothing special. On a stage or in front of a camera, I was somebody important. But in real life, I just didn't know how to deal with people. I was afraid if they realized how ordinary I was, they wouldn't be interested in me anymore."

Kitty shook her head in wonderment. That her father might have suffered from insecurities had never entered her mind. "Everyone I've met here thinks you're terrific. I don't know how many times I've been told nice things about you . . . about the real man, not the film star."

Mark grinned. "You know, it's funny. From

the day I bought this ranch, something changed for me. I don't know if it was coming here to my ancestral roots or whether I'd just outgrown Hollywood, but all of a sudden I wasn't interested in putting on an act anymore. I just started being me and for the first time actually liking myself. And when I no longer cared what sort of impression I made on other people, it turned out that most of *them* liked me too. All the same, none of it was enough until you came—not even Ellie. I really love you, Kitten."

"I love you, too, Dad," Kitty whispered.

"All right," Mark said in a brisk voice, "I've said my piece and I'm putting you on notice that I don't intend to lose you again. If you won't come here to visit anymore, Ellie and I will just have to go to you. Now let's discuss your plans. When do you intend to leave?"

"I'd like to go day after tomorrow if I can book a flight."

"So you're going to leave us, are you?" Ellie asked Kitty the next afternoon when she arrived at Mark's door.

Kitty nodded as Ellie came inside the entrance hall. "Tomorrow afternoon. Red will drive me to Dallas to catch the plane."

"Nonsense," Ellie said sharply. "I'll take you myself. We'll have a nice lunch together before you go."

"I'd really like that," Kitty answered. "Ellie, I'm sorry about upsetting your wedding plans, but—"

Ellie lifted her hand and gently interrupted

her. "Don't worry about it. It's a simple affair, as you know. It won't make a bit of difference except that we'll honestly miss you."

"Thanks. I appreciate your understanding." Kitty smiled. "Dad's really lucky to be getting you. You'll be good for him."

"Yes," Ellie said without false modesty. "I will be, because I love him. I'm only sorry things didn't work out for you and Josh. By the way, Adam told me he stopped by to see Josh this morning. Did you know he was ill?"

"He had a bad cough yesterday," Kitty answered. "What exactly did Adam say?"

Ellie shrugged. "His direct quote, actually, was that Josh looked like hell. He said he's feverish and chilled and coughing nonstop."

"Has he seen a doctor?"

"I doubt it. Most men are dreadful when it comes to taking care of themselves."

"Hey! Are you two going to stand by the door gossiping all day?" Mark yelled from the living room.

Both women laughed over the aggrieved tone in his voice.

"Coming, darling," Ellie shouted back. She looked questioningly at Kitty. "Are you coming too?"

Kitty shook her head. "I've still got some packing to do."

She went into her bedroom where her suitcase lay open on the bed. The truth was that there was little packing left to do, and what there was would take all of fifteen minutes to accomplish. But she was alarmed by the news about Josh, and she didn't want Ellie or Mark to see just how disturbed she was.

Now, as she tossed a sweater into the suitcase, Kitty tried to convince herself that Josh probably just had a case of the flu or even a simple chest cold. He'd be over it in a few days. Anyway, why should she care? Josh was nothing in her life anymore. Oh, sure, she loved him; but that was never going to change. Josh had told her bluntly enough that he didn't want her in his life, so what good would it do for her to worry about his health? Once she was gone, she wouldn't even be aware of how he was, so why brood about it now?

Telling herself it was settled, Kitty combed her hair and applied fresh lipstick. While Ellie was there keeping Mark company, she would drive over to say goodbye to Carol. It would be her last chance to see her and the baby, and, even more important at the moment, it would occupy her time and keep her from dwelling on Josh.

The hard, frozen ground crunched beneath Josh's boots as he walked from the truck to the edge of the water tank. His face was burning, a mockery of the penetrating cold air. Despite the sun that peaked through the blue-tinged clouds, the temperature hovered in the low teens. The cottonwoods, mesquites and pin oak tree branches were stark and bare, and clumps of prickly pear, killed by the freeze, drooped limply beneath patchy layers of snow.

Josh's entire body ached from exhaustion. A

tight band squeezed around his chest, and hourly it became harder to breathe. But he couldn't let up. Since the blizzard and the continued subfreezing temperatures, he'd been on a treadmill without relief: break the ice in all three water tanks every morning and try to see to it that the cattle drank; toss out some hay; search for dead or injured cattle; burn prickly pear; a quick lunch, if any at all, then back to the chore of chopping ice once more and checking on the cattle again before nightfall.

Gritting his teeth, he lifted the axe to his sore shoulder and swung it downward into the ice.

Minutes later, when he stopped to rest and catch his breath, he heard the sound of a vehicle. He jerked around and saw Mark's truck bumping along the tracks. It stopped beside his truck and Kitty jumped out. Her long, blue-jeaned legs moved swiftly as she walked toward him. Josh's eyes devoured the pleasing sight, and for one swift second he was conscious only of how glad he was that she was there.

Until he remembered. *No good,* his fevered brain reminded him. She didn't belong here. Too hard, too cold, too much work. Not for Kitty.

"What're you doing here?" he asked ungraciously.

Kitty tilted her head to one side as her dark eyes, assessing and critical, swept across his face. "Adam was right," she declared at length. "You *do* look like hell."

Josh scowled. "I've got work to do. I don't have time to waste listening to your opinion of me."

He turned his back to her, lifted the axe once more and, slicing downward, violently shattered the bed of ice.

An instant later, one of the horrible coughing spells that attacked him every few minutes came over him. Josh dropped the axe to the ground, reached into his pocket for his handkerchief and, as the seizure went on, doubled over. He was horrified that it was happening in front of Kitty, but he was powerless to stop it.

Kitty watched him with fresh alarm and knew then that her instincts had been right when, halfway to Carol's house, she had turned around and come to check on Josh after all.

The coughing ceased at last. Josh stood upright once more and turned slowly toward her. "You still here?" he asked harshly.

Ignoring his words, Kitty said, "You're sick. You've got to see a doctor. Today."

"I don't need a doctor. I'm fine." Josh bent and picked up the axe.

"You can't go on like this," Kitty said urgently. "What're you trying to do, kill yourself?"

"I'm trying to save my livestock. I've got too much to do to stop and pamper myself. I'm okay, so get the hell out of here, will you? Nobody invited you here."

"Josh, you . . ."

Before she could say more, he was consumed by a coughing spell even worse than the last one. Josh dropped the axe to the ground again and moved toward his truck. He leaned weakly against the bumper, as though he could no longer hold himself upright by his own power.

Anxiously, Kitty noted how red his face was one moment, how deathly pale the next. This time when the spasm ended, Josh didn't move. He slumped against the truck, eyes closed, gasping so hard for breath that Kitty could hear the rattling in his chest from where she stood.

She went to him and touched his cheek and grew even more alarmed. His skin was parched and burning. Josh opened his eyes and gazed dully at her, but she had the feeling he wasn't even seeing her.

"You're going to see a doctor," she said with an authority born of sheer terror. "I'll drive you."

Josh looked away from her toward the water tank. "The ice," he said helplessly. "The cattle . . ."

"I'll have Red and Oakie see to them," Kitty assured him. "One of them can drive your truck back to the house, too." She took his arm, urging him toward Mark's truck. "Let's go now. We need to get to town before office hours are over."

This time, to her vast relief, Josh didn't argue. He went with her meekly, and when she opened the passenger door, he climbed inside without protest.

The heater was soon going full blast, yet from the corner of her eye, Kitty saw Josh shiver. His face was still terribly pale, and his eyes were closed as his head nodded. It was as though once he had finally given in, he had totally collapsed.

After she'd closed the last pasture gate behind her, Kitty asked, "Who's your doctor?"

"Don't have one," Josh mumbled.

Kitty nibbled at her lip. "I'll have to ask Ellie

or Mark to recommend one. Is your phone working yet?"

He nodded, and Kitty sent heavenward a quick prayer of thanksgiving. She stopped the truck beside the house, leaving the motor and heater running. "Just rest," she said, "while I go in and call Mark. I'll be right back."

Josh didn't even appear to have heard her; he had begun coughing again. Kitty hurried to the house.

Ellie answered Mark's telephone and, when Kitty had explained the situation, gave her the name of her personal physician in Brownwood. "I'll call and tell them to expect you," she promised, "and if Oakie or Red can't see to the tanks, I'll call Adam. Tell Josh not to worry. We'll take care of everything."

"Thanks," Kitty said gratefully. She rang off and hurried back to Josh.

Josh dozed through the whole drive to Brownwood, and Kitty was glad. His breathing was still labored and raspy, but at least while he slept he wasn't having those awful coughing seizures.

Ellie had given her directions, and Kitty had no trouble finding the doctor's office. When they arrived, she woke Josh. "We're here," she said, gently shaking his arm.

Josh rubbed his eyes. "I don't need this," he protested. "I'm feeling a lot better since I had that nap."

"That's fine," Kitty said, "but since we're here, you'd better let the doctor look at you just the same."

Josh glowered at her. "Why don't you mind your own business?"

Kitty shrugged. "I will," she promised. "Later. When you're better."

Thirty minutes after Josh had gone into the examining room, a nurse came to the waiting room door. "Mrs. Peterson? Dr. Spellman would like to have a word with you."

Surprised, Kitty discarded the magazine she'd been thumbing through and followed the nurse into a private office. The doctor sat behind the desk, scribbling on a prescription pad. With his left hand, he waved toward a chair, and Kitty sat down.

When he had finished writing, Dr. Spellman said, "While Mr. Steele is getting dressed, I thought I should have a little talk with you. He has pneumonia."

Kitty gasped. It was worse than she'd thought. "Will he need to go into the hospital?"

The doctor shook his head. "I don't think we'll need to do that so long as he takes the antibiotics and stays in bed, but he'll need complete rest for at least a week." He smiled wryly. "The reason I called you in here is that he seems to be under the impression he's got a lot of work to do and can't spare the time for proper rest. He's a very sick man, and right now he's running a high fever. I wanted to make sure there was someone here to drive him home and see that he goes to bed and stays there."

"I'll see to it," Kitty promised grimly.

"Fine." Dr. Spellman handed her a prescription. "Have this filled. I don't anticipate any problems as long as he does as he's told, but if he seems to get worse, I'll expect to be called at once. Otherwise, I want to see him one week from today. And he's not to lift a finger before then."

Kitty stood up and nodded. "I understand. Thank you, Doctor."

Two hours later, just as dusk was falling, Kitty finally saw Josh into bed. He lay shivering beneath a mountain of covers as she spread still another quilt over him.

"I'm sorry," Josh murmured apologetically. "I'm making so much trouble for you. I've never been sick like this before. I don't know what to do."

Kitty smiled tenderly as she brushed his hair away from his feverish forehead. "I know exactly what you should do," she said softly. "Stop worrying and go to sleep."

Josh sighed and obediently closed his eyes.

Kitty stood watching him for another moment, and then, unable to resist, she bent and kissed his brow. Josh sighed again as she tiptoed out of the room.

There were no more questions or doubts in Kitty's mind. She knew precisely what she intended to do. She was going to stay in Texas and, if necessary, browbeat this man into marrying her.

Chapter Fourteen

Another storm system swept into the area that night, bringing more sleet and snow and record-setting cold temperatures. This storm was worse than the last because the winds were stronger and more destructive. Kitty was awake most of the night, tending frequently to Josh, and the sound of the violent storm as it battered everything that stood in its way kept her nerves on edge.

As the temperature plunged outside, Josh's seemed to rise. Arms and legs flailing, he tossed wildly in the bed and mumbled incoherently. He threw off his covers, claiming he was burning up, then went into convulsive shivers while his teeth chattered.

Kitty brought his medication when it was due and somehow managed to get it into him before he fell asleep again. Relieved, she covered him up, tucking the blankets around him, and was about to go back to her bed on the living room sofa when he grabbed her hand, sat upright in bed and exclaimed, "I'm late! I have to get to the auction! Where are your shoes?"

He was obviously hallucinating. "You have plenty of time for that later," Kitty said soothingly. "Why don't you take a nap first?"

"Plenty of time." Josh accepted the statement and fell back against the pillows. "Mom," he murmured as he turned his head restlessly, "Mom, you look so pretty in that dress. Where are you going? *Mother*, don't leave me!"

Kitty sat down on the edge of the bed and stroked his hand, as she imagined his mother might have done for her son had she been alive.

"I'm not going anywhere, Josh," she said softly. "I'm right here."

"Here," he sighed. "Did the letter come?"

"It came."

Josh sighed again and seemed comforted at last. Kitty stayed with him, holding his hand, until he finally drifted off.

The entire night passed in this manner and Kitty only managed to grab snatches of sleep. But by early morning the worst seemed to have passed. Both the storm and Josh's raging fever had broken, and as first light filtered through the windows, Josh sank into a deep, restful sleep.

Kitty made herself some coffee and opened the back door to look out. She was dismayed at what she saw. Part of the barn roof was on the ground;

a small tree had been uprooted and tree limbs and debris were littered everywhere.

Still dressed in the jeans and shirt she'd worn the previous day, Kitty slipped into her coat and went out to survey the damage. Close up, she saw that the barn was not as bad as she'd first believed. It could have been much worse. The house was intact, and though the lights had flickered throughout the night, they'd never lost electrical power entirely. The bitter cold made it difficult enough to keep the house snug and warm, but without power, they would have been in real trouble. As ill as Josh was, it might have been disastrous.

She returned to the house and had her breakfast, and when Josh awoke, she offered him some, but he fretfully refused. It was a real accomplishment when she persuaded him to drink a glass of orange juice.

The evening before, Kitty had telephoned her father and told him she'd be staying to care for Josh. Mark had been concerned and promised to have his hands make regular trips to Josh's pastures in his stead. He also promised to cancel her flight reservations and to send her clothes to her. She was not to worry about him. Even on crutches, he could manage to open a can of something to eat, he assured her, and during the daytime there would be the housekeeper or Ellie to look after him.

After Josh fell asleep once more, Kitty went out to check on the bridge. As she'd expected, it was slick, so she went to the garage, wrestled a bag of sand into the back of the truck and returned to the bridge to scatter it.

She'd scarcely finished when Adam and Oakie arrived, and they were able to cross the bridge without difficulty.

"How's Josh?" Adam asked Kitty when he stopped his truck beside her.

"He had a terrible fever all night and didn't sleep well at all, but it's broken now and he's resting better."

Adam's eyes were shrewd. "Looks like you could use a little rest yourself," he commented.

Kitty smiled. "Easy to say, but not so easy to find time to do. You guys want some coffee?"

"Better not," Adam said. "No rest for us, either. These storms are about to do everybody in. As soon as we finish Josh's work, we'll have to get back to our own." He opened the door of the truck and stepped out. "Almost forgot," he added. "Your suitcase is in back."

"Wonderful," Kitty said. "I'm dying to take a bath and get into some clean clothes."

The men headed toward the pastures while Kitty returned to the house. Josh had awakened and was calling for her.

"I'm thirsty," he complained. "Where were you?"

"Sanding the bridge. Adam and Oakie have come to break the ice on the tanks and feed your livestock."

Josh seemed lucid and nodded as though he understood. "Good," he said. "Good."

But three hours later, when he awoke another time, he was worried about his cattle and Kitty could not convince him that they had been tended. He insisted he had to do it himself, and it was all she could do to physically restrain him from getting up.

For three days the pattern was the same. Josh slept a great deal during the daytime, getting up only long enough to go to the bathroom and take a quick shower, which left him weak and shaken. He worried about his cattle whenever he was alert enough to remember, and complained that the juices Kitty brought him were not cold enough and the soups were too tepid. She was either smothering him with too many bed-covers, or she hadn't piled on enough. Like clockwork, late in the afternoon his temperature would rise and they'd face one more long night of broken sleep, hallucinations and fretfulness.

Daily he became more quarrelsome and disagreeable, and there were many times during those days of thankless work and constant complaints that Kitty had to bite back sharp retorts by reminding herself that Josh was only being impossible because he felt so awful.

On the third afternoon, after hearing one more time that she was lying to him about his livestock being cared for, Kitty hailed down Red and Oakie when they stopped at the pasture gate and had them visit Josh to reassure him themselves. Only after that did he cease to badger Kitty on that subject.

The following morning Ellie came. "How's it going?" she asked as she came inside.

Kitty grimaced. "It's the roughest job I ever

had. He's the most exasperating and impossible human being I've ever met!"

Ellie chuckled. "That much fun, hmm? I had a feeling that by now you might appreciate a friendly face."

"Do I ever! It's wonderful to have a nice, *rational* person to talk to."

Over coffee, Kitty was able to spill out some of her frustrations from the past few days, and then she caught up on the news about the wedding.

A half hour later came the familiar, plaintive call from the bedroom. "Kitty? Kitty, where are you?"

Ellie grinned and shook her head in sympathy as Kitty got up and went to answer the summons.

Josh was sitting upright against a stack of pillows, looking like one of the bad guys in an old Mark Winters Western movie. His face was dark with several days' growth of beard, and his hair, tousled by long, restless hours in bed, was also growing a bit long, curling wildly over his ears and brow and giving him a sinister appearance.

"I hear voices," Josh grumbled when she joined him. "Why didn't you wake me and tell me I had company?"

"You don't," Kitty said. "I do. Ellie's here. Can I bring you something?"

"Some water," he said. "My throat is dry."

Kitty turned to go, but when she reached the hall, he called, "I changed my mind. I want a soft drink."

Kitty returned to the door. "We're out. How about some apple juice?"

"I hate apple juice," Josh declared. "What else have you got?"

"Grapefruit or orange."

He grimaced. "I'm sick of both!"

Kitty kept her face deliberately bland. "Then have water."

"Isn't there any grape juice left?"

"Sorry." She was growing impatient. "Come on, Josh, what'll it be? Water or some of the juice we have on hand?"

"Neither," he snapped, in a sudden snit.

"Fine." Kitty shrugged and began walking out of the room.

"What's for lunch?"

"Chicken soup. Are you hungry?"

"Only a little, but I'm not in the mood for soup. Is there any ice cream?"

Kitty nodded. "Yes, there is, but that's hardly a meal. You need something to help you build up your strength. If you'll eat a little soup, then I'll bring you some ice cream."

"Damn it, don't talk to me like a child!" Josh exploded.

"Then stop acting like one," Kitty returned swiftly. "Do you want some soup now or later, Josh? Ellie's waiting for me."

He waved a hand in dismissal. "Then go," he snarled. "Go. Don't give me another thought."

When Kitty rejoined Ellie, the older woman was stifling a laugh. "Has he been that way all week?" she asked in a low voice as Kitty sat down and picked up her coffee.

There was a grim expression on Kitty's face as she nodded. "He gets worse every day."

"Then I think you must be some sort of saint to put up with him," Ellie said. "Or," she added thoughtfully, "a masochist."

Kitty shook her head and said ruefully, "Neither. I'm only a woman who loves him in spite of himself."

Ellie smiled. "Ah, I understand perfectly. Does this mean you're going to stay here after all and marry him?"

Kitty wrinkled her nose. "There's a slight hitch," she explained. "Josh has said he loves me, but because he thinks the rigors of ranch life would be too hard on me, he's also sworn he won't marry me."

Ellie frowned. "Hmmmmm, that could be a problem, all right," she allowed.

Kitty's face split into a wide, mischievous grin. "Not at all, actually," she said calmly. "It just might take a little time before I wear him down, that's all."

Her future stepmother threw back her head and laughed heartily. "I like your spirit, Kitty," she said. "And you know what? I'm betting on you."

Though Josh still felt weak the next morning, when he took his shower he managed to hang on long enough to shave as well. But the extra activity soon took its toll, and in shame, he had to crawl back into bed immediately afterward.

After lunch and a nap he felt stronger once more and, clad in his pajamas and robe, he tottered into the living room, where he eased himself into his recliner.

Kitty didn't seem to be around, so Josh picked up the newspaper that had arrived in the morning mail. He'd been completely unconcerned with current events the past few days and thought he'd enjoy catching up on the news, but for some reason the paper didn't hold his interest for long.

He tried to figure out what was different about the room. Kitty didn't appear to have made any real changes in it. The furniture all stood in the same places; the lamps were where they belonged; even his magazine basket was still right beside his chair. Yet somehow there was a difference.

After a while he realized what it was. The tables were spotless and polished to a high gloss; the throw pillows on the sofa were plump and inviting; the clutter of mail where he always tossed it on the lamp table was neatly stacked; even his high school rodeo and football trophies on the mantel gleamed with a new brightness. Kitty had changed nothing essentially—she'd just made everything better, more pleasant and comfortable. There was a cared-for look to everything that Josh had never managed to achieve with his hasty housekeeping efforts.

In short, the house looked as though it had a woman there who cared for it. Smelled like it, too, for he suddenly became aware of an enticing scent coming from the kitchen. Kitty was baking something and it smelled delicious.

A rush of winter air blew into the house as the back door opened. Beyond the breakfast bar that divided the rooms, Josh could see Kitty come in, remove her coat and run her hands through her hair. Then she moved out of sight, and he heard her opening the oven to check on whatever she was baking.

A minute later she came into the living room, but she didn't immediately see him as she turned toward the hall.

"Hi," he said.

Kitty swung around in surprise. "Well, hi. I was just about to check and see if you were still sleeping. You must be feeling better if you're sitting in here."

She smiled, and Josh's heart went soft as jelly. "I do," he said calmly, concealing the effect she had on him. "Except for this damned weakness, I feel enormously better. I think I'm about to rejoin the land of the living after all."

"I'm glad," she said simply.

There was a tiny silence as an awkward tension settled over them. Josh ended it by asking, "What smells so good?"

"Brownies," Kitty replied. "Want some?"

"Sure."

Kitty retreated to the kitchen and Josh stared broodingly into the fireplace, where cheery blue and golden flames leaped. He'd been unbearable the past few days, he knew. It was a wonder Kitty hadn't simply got fed up and walked out on him. He certainly wouldn't have blamed her if she had.

What would have become of him if that had happened? In all his life, he couldn't recall ever being sick beyond an occasional cold, and there had been precious few of them. He'd always felt a certain pride in his strength and vitality, yet here he was, as weak and shaky as a hundred-year-old man! No woman except his mother had ever waited on him or seen him in a helpless condition, and though he was genuinely grateful for what Kitty had done for him, he also felt very embarrassed.

Kitty returned bearing a tray with coffee and warm brownies. She served Josh and then sat down on the sofa to relax.

"I have a pet," she told him. Her eyes sparkled with excitement, animating her face, and Josh thought she'd never looked more beautiful. Which seemed odd, when he considered it, because Kitty wasn't wearing a speck of makeup, not even lipstick. Yet her skin glowed with a dewy freshness, and her cheeks and lips and the tip of her nose had a rosy touch from being outdoors in the cold air.

He wrenched his attention away from the soft, naturally red lips and tried to concentrate on what she was saying. "A pet? Did you take in a stray dog?"

Kitty shook her head and grinned. "A stray calf. Oakie found him on the highway day before yesterday. He doesn't have a brand or tags. Oakie asked around, but nobody seems to be missing him. He's still very young and has to be bottle-fed, so Oakie brought him to me and asked if I wanted to take care of him. He's so cute and lovable, Josh! He's got the prettiest little white face and big brown eyes and he comes running to cuddle up to me every time he sees me. I named him Baby and I'm keeping him penned in the yard and putting him in the barn at night. I hope you don't mind."

Josh frowned. He had to be realistic. He couldn't afford to indulge whimsy by making a yard pet out of a calf. It was one thing to nurse one until it was ready to be turned into the pastures, but quite another to give it a name and fall in love with it as Kitty had done. By the time it was grown, she'd be back in Chicago, and he'd be stuck with a spoiled calf that didn't know it was an animal!

"What happens when you leave?" he demanded, forcing himself to be stern. "Am I to play nursemaid to your stray and then be expected to keep a full-grown bull in my backyard just as though it were a dog or cat?"

"Of course not!" she exclaimed indignantly. "I'll take him over to Mark's, and Oakie will care for him."

"You know, don't you, that Mark isn't any more likely to make a pet of him than I would." His voice was kinder, but he didn't want her to be under any illusions. "We're cattlemen, Kitty. Livestock is our business, not our hobby. When he's big enough, he'll be turned out to pasture and later be sold at auction just like all the others."

Kitty clasped her hands together in her lap and looked down. "I know," she said in a small voice.

Josh hated himself for squashing her enthusiasm. He watched the smile fade from her face and felt like Scrooge at Christmastime. What had he accomplished except to make Kitty unhappy and to remind himself that she'd soon be leaving? Why had he felt it necessary to point out the inevitable fate of the calf? Just to hurt her?

Despite his weakness, he felt a surge of energy. He had a wild urge to go to her, to hold her, to smother her face with kisses until she smiled again.

But he had to maintain control so that the parting would be easier. And that meant hurting her again. Deliberately.

Josh sucked in a deep breath. "I'm feeling so much better," he said, "I think I can do without a nurse from now on. I really appreciate all you've done for me these last few days, but I know you must be anxious to get back to Mark's house, and I'm ready to manage by myself. If you'll go get my checkbook out of the top bureau drawer in my bedroom, I'll pay you."

Kitty's head jerked up as though an electrical current had shot through her. *"Pay me?* Pay me for what?"

"For your time, for all you've done this week." He saw the pain slash across her face. He wished he could snatch back the calculated, cruel words, but he restrained himself. He was doing this for her sake; he had to make her angry so that she would go away. It would be fatally easy to lower his guard and beg her to stay forever, but he couldn't allow her to do that to herself.

Kitty rose to her feet, stiff and ramrod straight. Her shoulders went back and her chin lifted with graceful dignity.

"And how much was it worth to you, Josh? The minimum wage? All you have?" She shook her head. "You told me once that I was hard and selfish where Mark was concerned, but you're no better. You've just insulted me deliberately because you can't admit to yourself that my love for you is real, that I had a right to help you because of it. Because then you'd have to let me into your life, and you're too selfish to do that. You'd rather force us both to face a future alone than take a chance on my love. Well, you win, Josh! I won't try to change your mind. As to what you should pay . . . you can't put a fair value on something that was done out of love. There is a price, but I'll let you figure it out for yourself."

Long after Kitty had gone, and the flames in the fireplace had turned to ashes, Josh sat motionless. Today was the first time she'd ever admitted she loved him. He'd known it, of course, ever since the day he'd told her he would never ask her to marry him. She'd been so hurt then, so wounded. As she'd been again today.

Still, he hadn't been completely certain. He'd had this dreadful suspicion that she had come to take care of him out of pity and a misguided sense of duty, because he'd been so alone.

Alone. As the afternoon shadows began to fall and the room took on a chill, the silence of the house seemed to echo the word, mocking him. The walls closed about him. Alone. Alone.

The price of a wrong decision, or of an unselfish love?

Chapter Fifteen

*M*ark was astounded when Kitty walked into the living room carrying her suitcase. "What're you doing here?" he asked. "I thought you were going to stay until after Josh went back for his checkup. That's not until day after tomorrow, is it?"

Kitty dropped her bag beside the door and sank wearily onto the sofa next to Mark's chair. "He said he could take care of himself now."

"Oh, I see. You had another fight."

"Not exactly, but he made it plain he didn't want me around anymore, so . . . here I am." Her chin quivered.

"Feel like talking about it, sweetheart?" Mark asked gently. "I mean about what's really wrong between you?"

Kitty met his gaze, and the love in her father's

eyes warmed her, melting some of the ice
around her heart. The night when she'd admitted to Mark that she loved Josh and wanted to go
away because of him, she hadn't, even then,
quite trusted him enough to confide in him. Yet
he'd turned the tables and confided in her the
reasons he'd always destroyed relationships in
the past. Today she truly needed someone, and
maybe this was the time really to become Mark
Winters's daughter, to pour out her pain to him
and lean on his strength.

"Everything's so twisted up," she began huskily. "In the beginning I put Josh off because I
was afraid of being hurt again, of being cheated
on and dumped again. After the way Bob treated
me, and what you did to Mom—" Mark winced,
and she rushed on hastily, "Please, I'm not
trying to hurt you now, honestly. Only to explain. All my anger over you and Bob put me off
close relationships with men. I convinced myself that all men were the same, that I was
better off without them. So when this thing
happened between Josh and me, I was afraid to
commit myself. He wanted me to stay here a few
months, to give us time to get to know each
other and see where our relationship was
headed." She shrugged expressively.

"And you said, 'Thanks, but no thanks,'"
Mark surmised quietly.

Kitty gave him a wistful smile. "That's right.
So, of course that hurt and angered Josh. At the
same time, he's had this fixation that because
I'm from the city, I must be very spoiled and

materialistic. I've never been able to convince him otherwise."

"That stems from the bad time he had with his fiancée," Mark told her.

"I know that, but Josh is judging me by what she did the same way I once judged him because of Bob. You see how ridiculous it all is? How many hang-ups we both have? We're a mess!"

Mark chuckled. "I have to agree."

Kitty glared at him. "It's not funny!"

"No, I know it isn't." Mark sobered at once. "It's just that when you reach my age, you see how unimportant some things are, how people create problems and obstacles without substance and bring about their own heartaches. I just wish you two could look beyond your noses, that's all, and see that the only thing that's really important here is how much you love each other and belong together."

Kitty shook her head. "We love each other," she said sadly, "but we don't belong together. For a while I thought we did. Even yesterday I was determined to get past Josh's resistance and make him realize it could work out if we got married, but today I saw that it never could. No matter how hard I tried to show him that I loved him, that I could be happy with a simple life, one that doesn't include meaningless fancy things, he just refuses to believe it. He's convinced himself that I'd be miserable."

She sniffed, fighting tears, and Mark said thoughtfully, "I guess this means you'll really be leaving soon."

Kitty nodded. "As soon as I can schedule a flight."

"Stay through the weekend," Mark urged. "I haven't had a chance to see you these past few days, and it might be many months before we see each other again."

Kitty's inclination was to hop onto the first plane heading north. But she couldn't hurt Mark that way. He was right; they'd been apart for most of the past week and it would probably be a long while before they were together again. Today was Wednesday. Even if she stayed until Monday, it wouldn't be much longer before she was gone.

"All right," she agreed. "I'll stay through the weekend."

"Good," Mark said with a satisfied smile.

To Kitty's surprise, the next couple of days passed swiftly. She drove Mark to Rising Star to visit friends, and the outing was good for both of them. Until the cast came off of his leg, Mark was entirely dependent on others to drive him around, and now that he was fully recovered from his other injuries, he was bored with staying at home.

On Friday evening they had a little dinner party that included Ellie, Adam and Carol. Everyone was so lively and in such good spirits that even Kitty felt more cheerful.

Saturday morning, leaving Ellie and Mark busily addressing three hundred wedding invitations, Kitty went with Carol to Brownwood. They'd decided to have one last shopping trip together before Kitty went home on Monday.

They dropped off little Adam at Carol's parents', and then they spent an enjoyable morning choosing wedding gifts for Ellie and Mark. Kitty chose a lovely silver tray, while Carol picked a crystal vase.

Over lunch, Carol said, "I really hate to see you leave, Kitty. You know, when you spent those days taking care of Josh while he was ill, I was sure you'd . . . well, you know. I just thought after that, you'd be staying permanently."

"Some things just weren't meant to be," Kitty said lightly. "Not everyone can be as happy as you and Adam."

"Well, they should be!" Carol declared. "We could have become really great friends if you'd stayed," she added wistfully.

"We *are* really great friends," Kitty responded with a smile. "The postal service still runs and the telephones still operate, you know. We'll stay in touch."

"I know, but it's not the same."

"No." Kitty suddenly felt melancholy. "It's not the same."

"Will you ever come back?" Carol asked. "I mean, in spite of Josh, Mark is still your father. Will you come for visits?"

Kitty nodded. "It's taken too many years already to get to know my father. Yes, I'll be back, but not for a while." Not, her heart added silently, until she was over a certain tall man with piercing gray eyes and a tiny white scar above his left eyebrow. Not until she felt she could see the gently rolling countryside without automatically thinking of him. Not until every winter storm ceased to bring his face to mind.

"How're you feeling?" Mark inquired. "You still look a little peaked."

"I'm fine," Josh said, brushing aside the concern as Mark entered the house, carefully manipulating his crutches. "Isn't Ellie going to come in?" He could see her sitting behind the steering wheel of her car.

Mark shook his head. "No. I can't stay long and I wanted to speak to you privately."

"If you're worried about the renovation of that Houston condo," Josh volunteered, "I've got the progress report here. I just talked with the manager and—"

"I didn't come about that," Mark said bluntly. "I came about Kitty."

Josh froze. "What about her?" Then, suddenly anxious, he blurted, "Has something happened to her?"

Mark nodded. "You happened to her." He smiled gently, but his words were firm. "My daughter is very unhappy and you're responsible for it. That doesn't please me, Josh."

Josh turned away from him. "Stay out of things that aren't any of your business, Mark," he warned.

"When Kitty is in pain, it is my business," Mark answered sternly.

Josh whirled. His eyes were narrowed and they glittered with unmistakable anger. "Oh, I get it," he said sarcastically. "After all these years, now you're playing the part of the doting, protective father and that gives you the right to interfere in my concerns!"

Mark winced, but he wasn't about to be deterred. "Okay, I deserved that, but yes, you're right. It does give me the right to be concerned."

"The hell it does!" Josh exploded. "I won't tolerate your meddling, Mark!"

"Maybe I should remind you," Mark said with a sudden touch of frost to his voice, "that I'm still your employer. I intend to say what I came here to say, and you're going to listen."

Fury darkened Josh's face. "I just quit!" he snarled roughly. "Now get out of my house before I throw you out!"

Mark went on as though the outburst hadn't occurred. "You look as miserable as my daughter does, and I don't like that any better. I love you like a son, Josh. My God, you must know that, so you can just stop glaring at me right now. Why don't you end this foolishness before you wreck both your lives?"

Josh's lips flattened over his teeth in a grim smile. "That's exactly what I'm doing—trying to keep from wrecking lives."

Mark shook his head. "You're sure going about it in a peculiar way." He paused, then went on quietly, "She's leaving Monday on the three-ten flight out of Dallas."

Kitty, leaving so soon! Josh was shaken by the news. He'd understood all along that she'd be staying until after Mark and Ellie's wedding.

Now it was to be Monday. Monday . . . and he'd never see her again. But then, that was what he wanted, wasn't it? What was best for them both?

"I see," he murmured at last.

"Stop her, Josh," Mark urged softly. "You need her, and you're a damned fool if you let her go."

Josh's jaw clenched. "You don't know what you're talking about!" he said flatly.

"Don't I?" Mark challenged. "After being a loser in love for so many years, I'm an expert on the subject. I've learned that it takes effort to make a relationship work . . . on both sides. Love, important as it is, isn't enough. You have to work at it. If you really do love Kitty, then you're as big an idiot as I was when I did nothing to stop her mother from walking out on me. Kitty's like Jeanne, loving and loyal and faithful . . . until you destroy it and prove to her that her faith has been misplaced. After that it's darned near impossible to earn it back again. If you lose her now, you'll lose her for good."

"Don't you think I know that?" Josh asked harshly. "But I can't give her the things another man might, the things you can, things she has a right to expect. I don't want her to feel deprived, and I sure as hell don't want my wife depending on her father to give her the luxuries of life!"

Mark chuckled. "Ah-hah! I thought we'd get down to the truth. You're willing to throw away a chance at real happiness for the sake of pride. What can I say, Josh?" He shrugged. "She's my only child and I intend to leave what I have to her when I go. But that's not going to stop her from being independent and self-sufficient now.

If having a lot of money and living lavishly were important to her, do you honestly think she'd be hurting right now? Or would she be congratulating herself on escaping a close call? Don't forget, Josh, she's seen the mess I made of my life in the past. I'm living proof that having more money than you need doesn't automatically guarantee happiness."

Monday morning dawned sunny and beautiful. Though it was cold, the temperature was well above the freezing mark and the day promised to be exceptional.

Josh went to the barn to feed Baby his calf formula. So far Mark's men had not come to fetch him, and Josh had been obliged to add nursing the young animal to his other chores.

The calf thrust his face against Josh with playful affection and Josh stroked his head. "You miss her too, don't you, Baby?" he asked. "But we'll just have to muddle along by ourselves. She's going home today."

All morning the knowledge lay heavily upon him. Kitty was leaving and he would never see her again. Already, the atmosphere of his house had changed. It had been warm, inviting, infinitely comfortable while she'd been in it, as though the very air had been charged by her presence. Now it seemed lifeless, dark, a cheerless place. Josh spent as much time outdoors as possible to avoid the sense of isolation and loneliness that now oppressed him whenever he was in the house.

Was Mark right? he asked himself as he

chopped wood. Was he condemning Kitty and himself to a lifetime of unhappiness because of mere pride? He didn't like to think so, but now he wondered. He loved her more than life itself, but he wanted her to have the best, not hardships and heartaches.

The pictures of her became sharp and clear in his mind: the glow on her face the day she'd helped Red and Oakie in the rainy pastures; the spirited independence she'd shown when she first saw Mark, to hide the love she really felt toward her father; her beauty and passion when they'd made love; that stormy night when he'd found her bravely working alone in his pastures, tending to the livestock. He remembered the nights she'd sat with him when he was running high fever. She'd held his hand, wiped his brow, and he'd fallen asleep to the reassuring sound of her voice. She'd seemed to take such pleasure in caring for him.

It suddenly came to him that Kitty really did like it there. She hadn't faked her pleasure at working in the pastures with Mark's men; she'd genuinely enjoyed herself. The night he'd found her in his own pastures, she hadn't been expecting him at all, yet she'd been working in a horrible storm as though it were her own cattle that were at risk. It was something you might expect a lifetime neighbor to do for you, but a young woman from Chicago? She'd done it because she'd really cared.

As for their own relationship, even after he'd told her he wouldn't ask her to marry him, she'd still come back when she learned he was ill

. . . and probably saved his life into the bargain. The care she gave him had been devoted and beyond what anyone might expect of someone who'd already been given her walking papers. For thanks, he'd told her a second time to go.

Well, he'd gotten his wish. In a few more hours she'd be gone for good. And he, fool that he was, wasn't lifting a finger to prevent losing the only woman in the world who mattered.

Smartly dressed in a navy wool suit and a crimson blouse, Kitty waited inside the passenger lounge at the Dallas–Fort Worth airport for her flight to be called. Mark and Ellie waited with her.

They'd arrived with ample time to spare after lunch in a nice restaurant, and now, through the wide glass windows, Kitty watched as the jet touched down, engines screaming. It sailed rapidly down the runway and out of sight.

"Right on time," Mark said with a glance at his watch. "It won't be long now."

"No," Kitty said hollowly. "It won't."

"Should we get you a magazine or something before you board?" Ellie offered.

Kitty shook her head. "No, thanks. I don't want anything."

The plane came back into view, nosing its way into position near the door of the lounge, and a short time later incoming passengers began straggling through it. "It looks like a full plane," Mark said, observing the packed lounge.

"Yes." Kitty's response was automatic; the truth was, she was uninterested. It had been a strain all day to keep up the polite conversation. She often found herself looking straight into Mark's or Ellie's eyes, honestly trying to pay attention to whatever was being said, but her unhappy thoughts kept returning to a man it was unlikely she would ever see again. She was so oblivious to everything else that not once had she caught the frequent exchange of worried glances between the couple.

All at once she was impatient to get on the plane, to be in the air, to be away from Texas. This brief interlude of her life was over, and the sooner she put it behind her, the better. When she got home she would immediately launch a search for a new job, try to get back her old part-time job at the exercise studio, perhaps take a night course of some kind and look up all her old friends. Activity was what she needed, a ceaseless round of it, so that she would have little time to remember. It might be years before the prescription took effect and cured her of a love that wasn't wanted, but she was determined to try. She had to pretend that other things mattered; otherwise, how could she possibly go on?

Kitty looked at her watch. Surely they would begin boarding soon. She opened her handbag, about to remove her ticket and boarding pass, when suddenly two strong, masculine hands gripped her arms and she was lifted from her seat.

Her handbag dropped to the floor as a familiar voice said urgently, "Kitty, I have to talk to you!"

In shock, she looked into Josh's face. His skin still had a slight pallor to it—a remainder, she supposed, from his recent illness—and his expression was one of anguish. Yet the strength of his fingers pressing into her arms was powerful, and his unwavering gaze was keen and intense.

"What are you doing here?" she gasped. Her mouth was dry as she took in the sight of him, a sight she'd come to believe she would never have again. He was dressed in a dark blue suit, his tie slightly askew, and his long, unruly hair still curled just above his ears and at his collar. But for all that, and in spite of his lack of color, he looked wonderful to her eyes.

"It's too crowded here," Josh stated. "Walk with me down the corridor. I have to talk with you."

Kitty swallowed hard and shook her head. For days she'd longed for this last goodbye, but now that it was here, she couldn't face it. It would be too hard to endure. "No," she said as coldly as she could manage. "They'll be boarding my plane any moment now. Besides, there's nothing left for either of us to say. It's all been said already." She caught her lip between her teeth. She had to keep strict control over her emotions so she wouldn't break down.

"There's plenty to say," Josh contradicted, "and you're going to hear it before you get on that plane."

"*Attention, ladies and gentlemen,*" a loudspeaker blared. "*We're now boarding Flight seven-eighteen, nonstop to Chicago. Children*

*and passengers requiring special assistance
should begin boarding at this time."*

Kitty tried to free herself from Josh's imprisoning fingers. "Let me go," she said in a low
voice. "That's my flight."

Josh shook his head. "You're not getting on it."

Kitty glared at him. "Have you lost your
mind?"

Josh grinned. "No. I think I finally found it
today. I'm not letting you go, Kitty. I love you
and I need you and I've come to beg you to marry
me."

Kitty's lashes swept up and her dark brown
eyes widened. "Did . . . did I hear you right?"
she asked faintly.

The loudspeaker crackled to life again.
*"Flight seven-eighteen for Chicago is now
boarding at gate six. Passengers seated in rows
ten through . . ."*

The rest of the speech was blocked out by
Josh's urgent voice. "I know I don't have a great
deal to offer you materially just now, but I'm a
hard worker, Kitty. I swear I'll make the ranch
pay off. I'll make you proud of me and give you
everything you deserve if only you'll marry me.
And," he added almost whimsically, "if Mark
will give me back my job."

"Give it back?" Kitty looked from Josh to her
father with confusion. "Did you fire him, Dad?"
she asked in disbelief. She had the horrible
thought that it was her fault, that her confes-
sions to Mark had caused him to dismiss Josh in
retaliation.

Mark didn't appear especially guilt-ridden, however. He grinned broadly and shook his head. "Actually, he fired me—for sticking my nose into places it didn't belong."

Josh lifted a hand and gently turned Kitty's face so that she had to look at him again. "Mark told me what a fool I'd be if I let you go because of my pride. I didn't listen to him then, but now I see how right he was. Kitty . . . darling, I love you. You must belong here after all, because otherwise why would my house be so empty without you? My *life* is empty without you. Why, even Baby misses you. Please come home. I know you've got doubts because of what happened in your first marriage, but it would never be like that with us. All I want in the whole world is the chance to love you every day for the rest of my life. If you can just bring yourself to stick out the rough places with me, someday I'll be able to give you all the nice things you ought to have and—"

"Your attention please. All passengers holding boarding passes for rows one through nine should board now."

"Damn!" Josh exclaimed. He threw a frantic glance toward the crowd of passengers lined up by the door. "I can't seem to talk fast enough."

Kitty laughed gently and lifted a finger to his lips. "You've said all I need to hear," she told him. "Josh, don't you realize by now that all I need is you? Just the security of knowing that, though good times and bad, you love me and will be there for me—that's all the riches I could ever want. I love you. I just want the chance to be with you and to share together whatever the future brings."

Josh sighed and his arms slid around her, drawing her close. "Oh, God," he murmured just before he kissed her. "I came so close to losing you."

Their kiss was long and deep, a confirmation, a promise, and it blocked out the entire world. Only when it ended and they heard Mark and Ellie's laughter and applause did they remember where they were and that they had an audience.

"Last call for passengers holding tickets for Flight seven-eighteen bound for Chicago."

"Here's your last chance to escape," Josh whispered huskily. "If you don't get on that plane, I'll never let you go away from me again as long as you live."

Kitty smiled dreamily and curled her arms around his neck. "You have to promise me one thing and then I'll stay."

Josh looked slightly anxious. "Anything within my power."

"That I get to keep Baby as my pet. He can be my wedding gift."

Josh laughed uproariously, then crushed her to him. "It's a deal, my love. So long," he warned, "as he doesn't receive more of your affection than your husband does."

"Never!" Kitty affirmed. Her lips brushed his lightly in promise.

"Suppose we should try to beat Mark and Ellie to the altar?" Josh asked in a low voice. "Or how about a double wedding on Valentine's Day? After all," he added with a tender smile, "Cupid kept on slinging those arrows at us until we got the message."

Kitty's throat tightened and she laughed huskily. "He did manage his task pretty well, didn't he? I can't think of anything I'd like better than to marry you on Valentine's Day—the same day my father at last finds his real happiness too."

Arm in arm, eyes glowing with the brilliant light of their future, they turned toward the smiling, older couple.

a fabulous $50,000 diamond jewelry collection

ENTER

by filling out the coupon below and mailing it by September 30, 1985

Send entries to:

U.S.
Silhouette Diamond Sweepstakes
P.O. Box 779
Madison Square Station
New York, NY 10159

Canada
Silhouette Diamond Sweepstakes
Suite 191
238 Davenport Road
Toronto, Ontario M5R 1J6

SILHOUETTE DIAMOND SWEEPSTAKES ENTRY FORM

☐ Mrs.   ☐ Miss   ☐ Ms   ☐ Mr.

NAME _____ (please print)

ADDRESS _____ APT. #

CITY _____

STATE/(PROV.) _____

ZIP/(POSTAL CODE) _____

RTD-A-1

RULES FOR SILHOUETTE DIAMOND SWEEPSTAKES

OFFICIAL RULES—NO PURCHASE NECESSARY

1. Silhouette Diamond Sweepstakes is open to Canadian (except Quebec) and United States residents 18 years or older at the time of entry. Employees and immediate families of the publishers of Silhouette, their affiliates, retailers, distributors, printers, agencies and RONALD SMILEY INC. are excluded.

2. To enter, print your name and address on the official entry form or on a 3" x 5" slip of paper. You may enter as often as you choose, but each envelope must contain only one entry. Mail entries first class in Canada to Silhouette Diamond Sweepstakes, Suite 191, 238 Davenport Road, Toronto, Ontario M5R 1J6. In the United States, mail to Silhouette Diamond Sweepstakes, P.O. Box 779, Madison Square Station, New York, NY 10159. Entries must be postmarked between February 1 and September 30, 1985. Silhouette is not responsible for lost, late or misdirected mail.

3. First Prize of diamond jewelry, consisting of a necklace, ring, bracelet and earrings will be awarded. Approximate retail value is $50,000 U.S./$62,500 Canadian. Second Prize of 100 Silhouette Home Reader Service Subscriptions will be awarded. Approximate retail value of each is $162.00 U.S./$180.00 Canadian. No substitution, duplication, cash redemption or transfer of prizes will be permitted. Odds of winning depend upon the number of valid entries received. One prize to a family or household. Income taxes, other taxes and insurance on First Prize are the sole responsibility of the winners.

4. Winners will be selected under the supervision of RONALD SMILEY INC., an independent judging organization whose decisions are final, by random drawings from valid entries postmarked by September 30, 1985, and received no later than October 7, 1985. Entry in this sweepstakes indicates your awareness of the Official Rules. Winners who are residents of Canada must answer correctly a time-related arithmetical skill-testing question to qualify. First Prize winner will be notified by certified mail and must submit an Affidavit of Compliance within 10 days of notification. Returned Affidavits or prizes that are refused or undeliverable will result in alternative names being randomly drawn. Winners may be asked for use of their name and photo at no additional compensation.

5. For a First Prize winner list, send a stamped self-addressed envelope postmarked by September 30, 1985. In Canada, mail to Silhouette Diamond Contest Winner, Suite 309, 238 Davenport Road, Toronto, Ontario M5R 1J6. In the United States, mail to Silhouette Diamond Contest Winner, P.O. Box 182, Bowling Green Station, New York, NY 10274. This offer will appear in Silhouette publications and at participating retailers. Offer void in Quebec and subject to all Federal, Provincial, State and Municipal laws and regulations and wherever prohibited or restricted by law.

SDR-A-1

READERS' COMMENTS ON SILHOUETTE SPECIAL EDITIONS:

"I just finished reading the first six Silhouette Special Edition Books and I had to take the opportunity to write you and tell you how much I enjoyed them. I enjoyed all the authors in this series. Best wishes on your Silhouette Special Editions line and many thanks."

—B.H.*, Jackson, OH

"The Special Editions are really special and I enjoyed them very much! I am looking forward to next month's books."

—R.M.W.*, Melbourne, FL

"I've just finished reading four of your first six Special Editions and I enjoyed them very much. I like the more sensual detail and longer stories. I will look forward each month to your new Special Editions."

—L.S.*, Visalia, CA

"Silhouette Special Editions are — 1.) Superb! 2.) Great! 3.) Delicious! 4.) Fantastic! . . . Did I leave anything out? These are books that an adult woman can read . . . I love them!"

—H.C.*, Monterey Park, CA

*names available on request